THE HOLDOUT IN THE DIABLOS

For two years Marne had trailed Lowden Doncaster, an unreconstructed Johnny Reb wanted for sedition and treason. Through cow camp and boom town, desert and border village, Doncaster managed to keep ahead of him, leaving Marne with only disturbing rumors . . . of guns and ammunition being cached along the Border . . . of a private army of outlaws and hardcases . . . of deals with renegade Indians.

But now at last Marne had caught up to him, and found Doncaster's secret Hole-in-the-Wall, and this time Marne was ready to trade bullets with the whole gang for a chance at Doncaster himself!

THE HOLDOUT IN
THE DIABLOS

Louis Trimble

GUNSMOKE

This hardback edition 2008
by BBC Audiobooks Ltd
by arrangement with
Golden West Literary Agency

ISBN 978 1 405 68187 2

British Library Cataloguing in Publication Data available.

Printed and bound in Great Britain by
Antony Rowe Ltd., Chippenham, Wiltshire

I

MARNE WAS WAITING for Doncaster. He crouched
in the shadow of an overhang of rock thrusting itself up from
the flat desert floor. The night was windless and the still,
warm air carried a confusion of sounds to Marne's straining
ears—the stirring of his horse picketed behind the rock, the
complaint of a coyote to the full moon, the echoing reply.

But the sounds Marne wanted to hear—the jangle of harness, the creak of saddle leather, the soft clop of shod hoofs
in the sand—these were missing. He relieved his cramped
muscles by standing briefly and then he settled back, a part
of the dark shadow that slashed across the sharp moonlight.
The night remained motionless. None of the high wind that
now and then scudded a thin cloud across the moon touched
the brush-dotted desert floor. Marne had the feeling that
the world was in suspension.

And this could be a futile vigil, he thought tiredly. A number of his Mexican friends just across the border to the south had passed on the rumor that Doncaster would be coming this way tonight. Even so, Marne found it hard to believe. The man had eluded him for two wearying, slogging years. And not once in those years had Doncaster even come close to committing a fatal mistake. Not once had he so much as let Marne, or any other hunter from the Provost-Marshal's office, get close enough for a look at him.

Yet his pattern of action was always the same. A sudden appearance followed by a seemingly wild running that might lead his pursuer from southern Colorado to west Texas. Then a disappearance as sudden as his coming. Two weeks, perhaps a month, would pass and then he would show up again.

Marne made a troubled sound deep in his throat. That had been the man's pattern for so long that his breaking it now made no sense at all. Why would he risk coming into this part of Arizona Territory? This close to Fort Douglas? What could there be for him here—except the danger of being captured, tried, and hanged? He had been charged with sedition and treason at the time of his escape from federal prison eight years ago, just after the war's end. He had done nothing since to lessen those charges.

A sound filtered through the soft air, brushing Marne's ear. He straightened his heavy-shouldered body, taking the kinks from his thighs, and then settled back against the rough rock of the overhang wall. He closed his eyes to rest them briefly and then stared out at the bright moonlight.

He heard the sound again—a hoof brushing sand softly—and now he saw the movement of a shadow blending and separating from the bushes scattered over the desert floor. The half muted jangle of harness caught his attention, and then the creak of saddle leather. The movement came closer, dead south of Marne now, coming up the trail from the Mexican border.

Marne lifted his carbine from its resting place by the rock wall. Carefully he cocked it, slowly so as to avoid the telltale snicking sound that could alert his quarry.

6

Now the rider was outlined against the night. He wore a nondescript outfit—a cowhand's wide-brimmed hat, a coat cut like a teamster's, trousers with a cavalry look about them. He rode slumped forward, and his horse moved slowly, walking the way a horse did when it had traveled too far without rest.

Marne waited until man and horse were abreast of the rock and less than twenty feet away. He stepped into the open and lifted the carbine to let moonlight glint off the barrel.

"You there. Pull up your horse!"

The slumped body straightened. Hands lifted high in the air. At the same time, the rider swung his horse with knee pressure and forced it toward Marne. He took two backward steps.

As he moved, Marne caught a sound from the far side of the rock overhang. He twisted about in time to catch the reflection of light from a raised gun barrel.

He swore at the trap he had stepped into so easily—letting himself be pulled into the open, his mind fixed on the one rider while another, most likely riding with muffled harness, came at him from the blind side.

Marne swung the rifle. He fired, forcing the man coming up from behind him to jerk to the left. Marne made a sudden run and dived into the shadow of the overhang. Two guns hammered against the night, and lead scoured the sand where he had been.

Marne rolled without dropping his gun, and came to his knees. He squeezed back into the darkness and peered forward. The man he had stopped was leaning out of the saddle, squinting against the blackness of the shadows. A sound to the right turned Marne that way. Whoever was there had left his horse and was trying to slide under the overhang on foot. If he succeeded, Marne would be pinned from two sides.

The man stopped moving. Marne frowned, wondering at the meaning of this. He swiveled his head, trying to keep

7

both the rider in front of him and the edge of the overhang under surveillance.

A voice came to him from the side. It was rich and deep, filled with the arrogance of a man sure of himself. "You," he commanded. "Move out where I can get a look at you. I want to see the man who's chased me for two years."

Elation surged through Marne. This was Doncaster! The rumors that led him here had been true. His hands shook a little as he shifted the gun. He had never been this close to his quarry.

He said thickly, deliberately roughing his voice, "The advantage is mine, not yours. You do the moving, friend."

"Two guns against one. You're whipsawed," the rich voice replied softly. "You can make it easy on yourself and maybe walk away from here, or you can be a fool—and rot in the sand."

Marne deliberately held a silence—as if he might be considering this. "What are your terms?" he asked finally.

"I want a look at you, army man. I want your name. And I want to know how you guessed I'd be coming this way."

"The answer to the last is easy," Marne said with soft mockery. He talked slowly, deliberately, shaping each word so that the tone of it was nothing like his own speech. Despite his pleasure in danger, his swiftness of decision when a move had to be made, he was basically a careful man. Until Doncaster was safely behind bars, Marne had no intention of revealing himself in any way that Doncaster might later identify.

"I'm here because you set a trap and I walked into it." It was a guess thrown out from the sudden flash of an idea. And Doncaster's amused chuckle confirmed the guess.

His voice sharpened suddenly. The amusement was gone, and the edge of it was as cold as honed hard steel. "Stop wasting my time, army man. Move out into the moonlight."

Marne shifted his rifle to his left hand, propping the butt on his hip. Now he was able to slide his handgun free. He took general aim with the carbine at the man in front of the

8

overhang and focused his attention on the right side of the rock.

He said tauntingly, "Come and get me, Doncaster."

A silence stretched long. Then Marne's ears caught the faint scuff of bootsoles sliding ever so lightly over the packed sand. He saw a flicker of shadow and judged the closeness of his man. He began to count the careful steps: "One," he said to himself. "Two." The next would bring Doncaster around the rock. But Marne knew that if he fired, the blast from his gun muzzle would make him a target for the man on horseback. His only chance was to try to fire the carbine with his left hand at almost the same instant that he fired the .44 with his right.

A bootsole stirred sand. Marne's mind whispered, "Three!"

His handgun ripped flame and smoke into the darkness. Before the sound had died, the carbine gave its hard, flat bark. He heard the .44 bullet scream agonizingly off the edge of the rock, sending razor sharp shards shrieking through the air. He heard Doncaster curse in surprise, stumble and twist backwards, away from the line of fire. Marne swiveled his head toward the man in the open.

He was half out of the saddle, his gun pointing down at the sand. As Marne watched, the gun blasted twice, sending up spurts of dirt. Then it fell free and the rider followed it awkwardly, slowly, until he was on the ground. He came to one knee and stayed that way, his head hanging.

Dropping the carbine, Marne stepped toward the right side of the overhang. He moved cautiously, hugging the rock wall, easing to the edge, trying to catch the sound of Doncaster's movements. Then he heard the jangle of harness, the creak of saddle leather. He stepped abruptly around the rock. His gun was up, but he let it fall to his side as he saw Doncaster spurring a long-legged horse away into the night. He sent the animal weaving through the harsh moonlight, making a deceptive target; and with each stride he drew farther and farther out of handgun range. That he had run away puzzled Marne until momentarily Doncaster was caught and held by the moonlight. He rode with a handkerchief held to one side of his face. Cut, Marne guessed, by the flying shards of rock.

Marne stood motionless, swearing helplessly, watching Doncaster race away into the night. For more times than Marne liked to recall, Doncaster had evaded a trap, leaving his hunter emptyhanded.

II

MARNE LIFTED his handgun and let it fall with a sour grunt. Except for that brief instant when he had revealed himself, Doncaster had handled his horse and himself in such a way that he made an impossible target. With the carbine, he would have had a chance to pick his man out of the saddle, Marne knew. But it lay where he had dropped it in the overhang.

He turned back to the wounded man. He had not moved, and when Marne came close he did no more than lift his head. He revealed a long, bony face, a drooping mustache over a heavy, loose mouth, and a long scar that ran up his sunken cheek to pull down his left eyelid. He was no one Marne recalled ever having seen.

"Doncaster ran out on you," Marne said softly.

The loose mouth made an effort to twist into a grin. "Ain't that hell." His voice was thin and pain-caught.

"Where are you hit?"

"Shoulder. That was a lucky shot of yours."

Marne walked to the man's horse and pulled his rifle from its boot. He picked up the gun lying on the sand and made a hand motion toward his prisoner. "Get on your horse."

"Go to the devil."

Marne said, "Put a bandanna over the hole in your shoulder. That'll do until we get to the fort. Now move."

The man stayed where he was, grinning tauntingly. Marne said, "You can ride sitting in the saddle or belly down across it. Take your choice."

The man moved now, but with deliberate slowness. He made a clumsy bandage from his bandanna and then lifted himself into the saddle. The movements sent a spasm of pain across his bony face.

Marne stood aside and directed his prisoner around to where the buckskin waited. Lifting himself onto the horse, he pointed to the northwest.

"It isn't more than an hour's ride," he said. "Start your horse."

"You haven't much feeling for a man's troubles," the other observed. He kicked feebly at his tired horse's flanks.

"That depends on the man," Marne answered. "I see people as different from animals because they can choose between right and wrong. When a man deliberately chooses wrong, I can't feel much compunction toward him."

"Wrong is a matter of opinion," the man said.

"Not when it means going to Doncaster's side—knowing what that will lead to in the way of families killed, people made poor, land laid waste."

The man laughed roughly. "What are you, the chaplain at Fort Douglas? Who are you to call Doncaster evil?"

"I'm the man who's been tracking him for two years," Marne said. "I've seen what he's left behind him."

The man was silent and Marne said no more for some time. Then he saw that his prisoner was beginning to weave in the saddle and he rode alongside, an arm ready in case the man should begin to fall.

Marne said abruptly, "How did Doncaster know he was riding into a trap? Who told you someone was waiting back there for him?"

"Nobody," the man said thickly. "He's careful, that's all. When he saw that rock sticking up out of nothing, he judged it safer to act as if it was a trap."

Marne didn't believe him. There were too many along this stretch of border country who might have guessed his reasons for asking questions, and who would have enjoyed passing their guesses on to Doncaster—border banditos, Indian rene-

11

gades, drifters of one sort and another. Besides, he had Doncaster's own laughing admission.

He said, "What did Doncaster want badly enough to come this close to Fort Douglas to get?"

"Find him and ask him," the man gibed. He let his head drop forward. He rode that way, his hands clasped loosely around the saddle horn, his body slumped as if in sleep.

Neither man spoke again until they reached the Fort. There Marne turned his prisoner over to a sergeant and rode quickly to the Colonel's quarters. Late as it was, he expected the Colonel to be waiting. He was—drinking strong coffee and chewing on one of his thin, dark stogies.

He indicated the coffee pot as Marne stepped inside and saluted. "Success, Captain?" He thrust his lean, sharp features forward. "No—I can see the answer by your expression."

"I brought in a man but not the right one. He and Doncaster tried to whipsaw me—and they nearly did." He sketched the story briefly.

"Did Doncaster have a good look at you?"

"No more than before," Marne said. "I was in shadow most of the time. I can still keep hunting him, if that's what you're wondering."

"This other man, did he see you?"

"A few glimpses. But it doesn't matter. He doesn't have my name. Besides, we can keep him in the stockade on a number of charges."

A knock came on the door. A young, fresh-faced Lieutenant stepped inside, saluted, and said in a half surprised voice, "The man the Captain just brought in is Private Carnap, sir." He nodded a greeting at Marne.

"Carnap!" the Colonel murmured. "He escaped from the stockade two—no, three months ago."

"Almost three, sir. He escaped early in February." The Lieutenant frowned. "He has a bad shoulder wound, but the doctor said we could question him by tomorrow."

"I'll take charge of the questioning, Lieutenant." The

Colonel dismissed him with a gesture. When the door had closed, he looked back at Marne. "Killian is a little eager. He was in charge the night Carnap broke out."

"I must have been away when he was stationed here," Marne said. "I don't recognize the face or the name."

The Colonel nodded. "Carnap was only with us a few months—a recruit—when we found that he was sending out information we were gathering on Doncaster. He seemed to have a number of friends among the renegade Indians in these parts. We locked him up, but the damage was done."

Marne grunted. "Then Carnap could have been the reason Doncaster never stepped into any of the traps we set this past winter."

"He probably was. He's not a literate man, but he's no fool." The Colonel frowned. "But that doesn't explain what happened tonight."

"Tonight just gives us more proof of what we've been sure of for some time," Marne answered. "That Doncaster has built an efficient and dangerous organization these past years."

The Colonel nodded, but his expression was gloomy. "As long as all we have to go on is educated guesswork and rumors, we'll never convince them back in Washington. The answers to my last reports all said about the same thing: There hasn't been a war on for eight years and it's about time we stopped chasing unreconstructed Johnny Rebs—including Lowden Doncaster.

"People do a lot of forgetting in eight years," he added sourly.

Anger pulled down the corners of Marne's mouth. "Damn it, sir," he said thickly, "what does Washington want? They know there are still a lot of homeless, rootless southerners in the west, and even more northern soldiers who've never been able to find a place in society since the army turned them loose. These are the kind of men Doncaster is pulling to himself, the kind he'll make use of when he's ready to hit."

The Colonel gulped coffee. "I know all the arguments, Curt. I've pointed out to Washington that you speak Spanish

13

like a native and that you've heard a good many stories from Mexican friends along the border. I told them of the rumors you picked up about wagonloads of war surplus guns and ammunition disappearing into Mexico but not showing up there anywhere, and of the stories of men drifting into the country and disappearing."

He set down his empty cup and touched a match to his tired stogie. "Washington has as good as ordered me to stop wasting time, money, and men. They left the door open with the usual remarks about my getting solid proof.

"If I could get some, I'd act now and get permission later," he added very softly.

"What is their idea of solid proof?" Marne demanded. "Doncaster and his men raiding Arizona and New Mexico Territories? Taking land and cattle from the new settlers? Taking money from the little banks starting up? Arming the Indians and turning them loose on us?"

"You don't have to convince me," the Colonel said mildly. "I know what a man like Doncaster can do if he isn't stopped before he gets his armies moving."

He poured himself some more coffee, turned to Marne, and said suddenly, abruptly, "I'm sorry it had to end this way, Curt."

Marne stared at him. "End? I'm not finished, sir. Just because Doncaster got away again doesn't mean . . ."

"I'm talking about official orders from Washington," the Colonel said. "They're very considerate of my officers. They pointed out that you haven't had one real leave in the eight years you've been in the Provost-Marshal's office. And they've ordered that you take leave now—a long one." He glared at his coffee cup. "They don't give me any loopholes. Not a one!"

A broad grin was stretching Marne's features. He chuckled and then burst out in solid laughter. The Colonel stared at him. "Maybe Washington is right. You do need a leave." His voice became cold, formal. "What is so amusing, Captain?"

Marne choked back his guffaws. "You can report, sir, that I'm taking my leave as ordered." He laughed again. "What

I do with my time while on leave is my personal business. Washington has nothing to say about it."

"Meaning you'll use the time to continue hunting for Doncaster?"

"Yes, sir. I want to try something different. I'm going into Mexico, to try and follow those wagons full of guns and ammunition. If I can find out where they went, I'll find the headquarters of Doncaster's organization. And I'll find Doncaster."

"Alone?" The Colonel shook his head. "No," he said flatly. "It's too dangerous, Curt."

Marne's smile took the sting out of his answer. "When I'm on leave, your orders won't have much force, sir."

"Don't forget that Doncaster had a trap set for you tonight," the Colonel snapped. "If he suspects that the army is still on his trail, he'll set another one. And if you happen to be near his headquarters, it won't be any simple two man affair like you ran into tonight."

"I'll keep it in mind," Marne said dryly.

The Colonel glared at him. Then he said in his crisp, official voice, "Let me warn you, Captain—if you find yourself in trouble, don't turn to us for help. Nor to a local lawman. From now until you report for duty again, you're not acting for the government.

"You're on your own. And the only law you can turn to is the law you make yourself."

III

CLEAR TRACKS from a heavily laden wagon train kept Marne moving doggedly north across Mexico's Sonora desert. The sign left by the wagons was a good six weeks old, but it was still easily readable in sandy dirt that had seen nothing but blistering sun since early spring.

Now it was well into June. Both Marne and the slab-sided

15

dun horse he had selected for this trip were baked dry by more than a month of steady, grinding heat. He had ridden as far south as the mining country around Parral before rumors and, finally, the tracks of the wagon trains had turned him north again.

Over a month, Marne thought. Nearly five weeks for Doncaster to whip his men into shape, to get ready to make his move. And he would move soon, Marne was sure. The fact that it had been a full six weeks since the last wagon had swung into Mexico and then turned north again was frightening. It could only mean that Doncaster had finally gathered all of the supplies his army would need.

Marne rode now with his head down, letting the slanting sun batter the top of his five gallon hat instead of his bearded face. Except for the untrimmed beard, he looked the part of the drifting cowhand he claimed to be—jeans and leather vest, full saddlebags and a lumpy warbag lashed on behind his cantle. His growing up on a ranch in the high country of southern Colorado had given him a cowhand's trade. The week before, he had helped for three days on a Mexican round-up and no *vaquero* there had questioned his handling of the stock or his easy, fluent border Spanish.

He grunted as he stopped the dun and reached for his canteen. A lot of use his cowhand training or his use of another language would be if these wagontracks didn't lead him to Doncaster. But if the rumors were true, the tracks would take him to where both his skill with a rope and with Spanish could do him some good.

They could keep him alive, he thought—as long as no one suspected he was an army man.

He sucked a little warm water from his canteen, poured a few drops in his cupped palms and gave it to the horse. Then he mounted and they slogged on again. Only the wagon sign unwinding endlessly northward kept Marne beating himself and the dun against the desert at this time of year—only the tracks and the growing sureness that the rumors were right, that he knew where those deep ruts were leading him.

And when Marne lifted his head he saw the mountains—the strange upthrust that appeared to break the empty flatness of the northern horizon. He slapped the dun's neck, raising a cloud of pale tan dust.

"Look there!" Marne croaked. "See those peaks, fellow! Those are the Diablos. And that's snow. Below them is timber. Trees and cold water creeks and cool high country air for us tomorrow!"

He laughed at himself for the sudden excitement that shook him. But it was more than just the knowledge that the tracks were leading him into the Diablos, where he would find relief from the sun and the heat. Now he was as sure as if Doncaster himself had told him so that the man's headquarters would be there.

The perfect place, Marne thought. In the United States but not really of them. Isolated, yet only a short forced march from the main road running west across New Mexico Territory to Arizona and California beyond. Inhabited, but with only a handful of people, and those not interested in the outside world, wanting only the peace and contentment of their hidden valleys.

Marne squinted at the Diablos through the shimmer of heat haze. They were strange mountains, rising up suddenly to straddle the border between Mexico and New Mexico Territory. Spawned by some ancient convulsion of the earth, they seemed little touched by the eons of weather that had worn the land around them to desert flatness.

Mountains of the devils, the Indians had called them, and the Spanish had taken over the name when they established silver mines there over two hundred years before. And, Marne knew, they were still mountains of the devils to most Indians, few of whom would ever venture into them.

According to ancient legend, an entire tribe had been trapped in the mountains while fleeing from an enemy people. They had been in the very heart of the high country when evil spirits had sent the land into wild convulsions. When it had settled again, the Indians found that there were only two ways they could get back to their familiar flat country—both narrow trails easily blocked by an enemy. And that enemy was waiting to wipe all but a handful of them out.

Marne could well believe the old legend after his three weeks of wandering through the Diablos. He had been on Doncaster's trail then, almost two years ago. The signs of the earthquake that had torn the land were almost hidden by grass and trees but even now only a few trails led in and out. A man could come up from the Sonora desert two ways, one of which was not always possible for a man on foot, let alone on horseback. And he could get north into New Mexico Territory by only one trail. On the east and west sides, sheer cliff faces and deep canyons blocked his way. And once at the bottom of the cliffs, he would have only trackless, heat-warped desert facing him.

Marne recalled how often in those three weeks he had lost his man in the maze of twisting narrow canyons and faint trails, half of them dead ends. It would have been then—two years ago—that Doncaster realized that the Diablos were perfect for his headquarters.

Marne wondered how Doncaster would have handled the willingly isolated people of the one tiny settlement. It was a village of people descended directly from the long gone Spanish silver miners and their families. They ran cattle in the few grassy valleys; they worked the played out mines occasionally, and they raised hay and root crops along the river. Now and then they freighted hides and ore to El Paso and brought back those things they could neither make nor grow—ammunition and guns, coffee and cloth and liquor. But for the most part, they tried to keep their independence, their freedom from the swiftly expanding world to the north of them.

Those he had met had been hospitable, Marne recalled. Especially old Manuel Potrero, the mayor and sheriff and general leader of the settlement. Manuel and Mike Farrel, the Irish trader who had wandered in years before, married Manuel's eldest daughter, and stayed to rebuild and run the ancient posada, the inn with its half dozen sleeping rooms, its dining room, and its cantina. Marne remembered them the best.

He slapped the dun, again raising a spurt of dust. "Move, fellow. I know where there's a spring and thick grass and good dry wood."

By dusk, Marne could feel the coolness rolling down from the snow-covered peaks. The tracks had led him to the southwest corner of the Diablos, and now he could see the sign climbing on up the twisting trail that slashed pale brown against the black slag of the lower slopes. It was more than a trail now, he noticed; it was a road. A road widened to take the heavily loaded freight wagons that had obviously been coming this way for some time.

The temptation to ride the broad trail was strong, but Marne thrust it away. If he was right, if Doncaster's organization was centered in the Diablos, then he would be sure to have guards posted somewhere above. And Marne wanted to slip unnoticed into the mountains—at least in the beginning.

He sought to recall the other trail. Two years ago, he had started up it and had been forced to turn back. Time and weather had made it virtually impassable for a man in a hurry. Great chunks had been torn out of the trail where it slid along cliff faces, trees and boulders were heaped over it, and at the top, instead of a notch through the peaks, there was a great rounded shoulder of rock to cross.

Marne patted the horse. "But," he murmured, "unless that trail's been improved, Doncaster won't be bothered to have a guard posted along it."

It was worth taking the time to try, Marne decided. He rode eastward along the base of the mountains, stopping when he reached the spring he had been longing for. For the first time in over a week, Marne and the dun drank their fill. He celebrated with an extra slab of bacon and an extra pot of coffee. With the dun picketed on grass growing behind the spring, Marne sprawled against his saddle and placidly smoked his pipe. Tomorrow's problems would have to look out for themselves. Tonight, he intended to suck all the pleasure he could from this cool, well watered camp.

In the early morning light, the east trail had a deceptively easy look about it. The beginning slope was gentle enough, as were the first kinks that carried Marne and the dun up across the face of the black lava rock forming the lower hills. But at the end of the lava the trees began—and so did Marne's troubles. By evening, he was only halfway to the great upthrusting shoulder of rock that marked the border between the two countries. Both he and the horse were slogging now, exhausted from fighting their way over deadfalls, climbing rubble heaps where a trail had once been, and in one place skirting a chasm on a rock ledge less than two feet wide. Marne had walked more than he had ridden, and he made camp when he found a small spring, wanting the water to soak his aching feet.

The next morning showed him a trail that was in worse condition than the stretch he had managed to come over. But after a half mile of obstacles, the road ran open and easy to the foot of the high rock shoulder. Marne reached it by noon, stopped for a quick, cold meal, and then left the dun and went forward on foot to see what condition the trail was in. Supposedly it skirted the huge, barren slope of rock, but some catastrophe had torn great chunks of trail from the cliff face and hurled them out of sight into a canyon.

Marne returned to the horse and studied the curve of the rock shoulder. It could be ridden, he decided. But if anyone was on guard on the far side, he would be a prime target once he was on the other face of the curve.

He managed to ride the dun most of the way. Only near the north end of the crossing was the slope too steep for him to trust the horse's footing; from that point he led the animal.

Beyond the rock, forest-covered level land stretched for a good mile. Beyond the timber was a series of low rises. After them, the land sloped sharply down toward the first of the narrow valleys that were so characteristic of the Diablos.

Marne heard the rifle shots as he approached the last rise. He dropped quickly out of the saddle and pulled the dun back into a tiny, tree-rimmed meadow he had recently passed. Taking his carbine from the saddle boot, he moved forward again. As he neared the top of the far rise, he went belly down in the grass and wormed his way forward Indian fashion.

Below him the ground dipped abruptly, plunging in a long, rubble-covered slope to the green depths of the valley. The shooting was coming more steadily now and Marne located it below him and to both the right and left.

He squirmed forward cautiously. Less than fifty feet below, a man lay on his belly. A gnarled juniper root pressed against his chest kept his body from sliding down the rubble. But each time he moved in an attempt to answer the rifle fire probing up at him from below, dirt slid from under his middle and rattled down in a miniature landslide.

Marne unslung his field glasses and brought the man on the slope into focus. He swore in surprise. But there was no doubting the owner of those sun-scorched, freckled features. It was Lieutenant Tim Killian. Marne had seen him last in the Colonel's office, well over a month ago. What the devil was one of the Colonel's staff doing here?

Then a puff of smoke below and to the left swiveled Marne in that direction. He had a quick glimpse of sunlight on the steel of a rifle barrel. Lead whined off rock near Killian, sending his head ducking down. Another shot snapped sharply from below and to the right, and shards of rock spat at Killian's face. Marne swore. Whoever the men below were, they obviously had Killian pinned on that slope. Without help, he could never climb the fifty feet and live.

Marne cupped his hands to his mouth and made the raucuous, scolding sound of a mountain jay. He saw Killian's head come up and then drop down again. Marne repeated the sound, this time holding the last note unnaturally long. It was a signal Killian could not miss. The head came up again and started to turn.

Marne called softly, trying to roll his words along the slope, "Can you get up here if I cover for you?"

Killian ducked his head as a rifle put lead close to him. "Who the devil are you?" he called.

"Keep it quiet," Marne called. "They haven't seen me yet."

He moved his gaze to the big rocks at the foot of the rubble slide. Only now and then could he see the men moving behind those rocks. But as he lifted his gaze out across the valley, he made out three specks rapidly growing larger.

"Make your move," he called. "They're getting help."

Killian held motionless for a long moment. Then both rifles probed toward him. He twisted his head toward Marne. "Cover me!"

Marne rose to his knees and lifted his carbine. He snapped a shot downslope to his left, swung the gun and sent lead whining off the rock to the right. He knew that he was exposed and he dropped flat as the man on the left recovered and fired. But the upward angle was a difficult one and the bullet came nowhere near Marne. He drove the man on the left to cover with a quick shot and then aimed to the right again. He had a brief glimpse of Killian rearing up, rolling over, and starting up the rubble slide on his hands and knees, gun slung over his back now.

Marne held his fire, swiveling his head quickly from one side to the other. He dared not waste lead. In the time it would take him to reload, they could get Killian, helpless as he was now. At the same time, Marne knew that he had to keep both snipers continually off balance.

Sunlight gleamed on metal to the right. Marne moved his carbine and fired. The man on the left had a bead on him now and his bullet sent a small animal scurrying in fright from a nearby bush. Marne drove a shot to the left. The man on the right nearly caught Killian as he reared up to thrust himself forward. Marne forced the man back into the protection of his rock.

Killian had cut the distance in half. "Hurry it!" Marne urged. He saw the man on the right run into the open and kneel to get a better bead on Killian. He fired and grunted with pleasure as his bullet ripped the rifle from the man's hand. His shout was audible to the top of the slope as he clamped his torn hand under his armpit and ran behind the protective rock.

Now Marne could concentrate on the man on the left. Once he risked a glance into the valley and saw the three specks had become horses and riders. They were almost within rifle range now.

"Move!" Marne snapped. He fired downslope. Once. Twice. A shot answered, driving a bit of razor-edged rock at Killian's face. He swore and scraped a hand over the sudden thin spurt of blood. Then he was at the top of the long slide and flopping like a played out fish at Marne's feet.

Marne snapped, "Keep going up the hill," and sent two quick shots downslope. But now both men had stopped firing. They disappeared into the rocks, and a moment later appeared again but now on horseback. They spurred together eastward along a trail running through the valley.

Marne was puzzled as to their reasons for going away from Killian. Then he saw the other riders coming west along the trail. Marne lifted his glasses and the riders seemed to rush up at him.

There were three of them. The man in the lead slouched on a strapping black horse. He was powerful looking even with his shoulders humped forward and his head dipped. As the two riders came nearer he raised his head and Marne saw the heavy features, the mouth covered by a drooping black mustache. It was no one Marne knew and so he turned his attention to the rider a half pace behind.

He sat astride a pale golden horse, erect in the saddle. Tall and finely built, he held himself so that the afternoon sun glinted off a reddish blond beard to show the sharp carving of his profile. Marne had a desire to shout his pleasure. There was no doubt at all. Beneath that beard were the unforgettable features of Lowden Doncaster.

Behind Marne, a tired voice said quietly, "I don't know who you are. But unless those are friends of yours down there, you'd better start moving. There's a trail leading up here, and it won't be long before they're on it."

Marne turned and looked into Killian's dirt- and blood-smeared features. The Lieutenant added, "The only trouble is, we haven't any place to go. Once they're up here, they've got us boxed. And this time there're five guns against us."

IV

MARNE GLANCED into the valley. The pair who had been shooting at Killian had joined Doncaster and the heavyset man on the black horse. A fifth rider came up quickly from the rear and joined them. All five headed along the trail for the east end of the shale slide.

Marne started south. Killian fell into step alongside him. Marne said, "Where's your horse?"

"Dead at the bottom of the shale slope," Killian said. "That's why I was caught that way. Tink and Smitty shot my horse out from under me."

"Tink and Smitty—the pair we chased out of the rocks?"

"They're Carl Rutter's men," Killian explained. "He's the joker on the black horse. He supposedly runs the CR ranch. It's in the second valley over. But . . ."

He stopped abruptly and swung in front of Marne. "Look," he said, "you saved me but I still don't know . . ." He broke off a second time. "Captain Marne, by God!" He lifted a hand to salute.

"Forget the ceremony and forget the title," Marne said sharply. He turned toward the meadow where the dun waited. "What are you doing here? The Colonel told me that the Doncaster case was officially closed."

"It is," Killian said. "But a week after you left, Carnap escaped again. I was assigned to go after him. He led me here—right to Doncaster's front porch. His wound slowed him down and made him careless."

Marne glanced back toward the valley. "It looks like he led you into a trap," he said dryly.

Killian shook his head. "I've been here almost three weeks," he said. "They didn't know who I was until today."

They reached the dun. Marne wondered how far it could carry them both. He said, "As I recall, there's a cut-off trail running over to the wagonroad that comes up from Mexico. If we can get on that before Doncaster and his crew reach this flat, we have a chance."

Killian shook his head. "There are men stationed on the wagonroad just north of where the cut-off comes in. They keep a constant watch on it. And another crew where the road starts down to the New Mexico desert. Frankly, Captain, I don't know any way out of here."

Marne said harshly, "I told you to forget the title." He motioned for Killian to climb aboard the dun. He followed and headed the horse slowly back toward the big rock shoulder.

"If the trails are so well guarded, how did you get into the Diablos?"

"I had a bit of luck," Killian admitted. "I saw the guards on the wagonroad before they saw me. I hid until dark and then tried to ride through them. I almost made it, but near the little town—Arroyo Verde—I went over a cliff and bruised myself up pretty badly. I cracked some ribs, banged up a leg, and had a concussion. I managed to get into the town."

He laughed harshly. "I'd read your report on how hospitable everyone was there. Well, I found exactly two people with the courage to help me. A girl named Marita Farrel and her cousin Tonio Potrero. She owns the inn and he helps around the place. And they had to keep me hidden or the others—including her grandfather the sheriff—would have turned me over to Rutter's crew. They were looking for me, with orders to shoot on sight."

"Potrero is afraid of this Rutter?"

"Along with everyone else in these mountains," Killian affirmed. "But nobody—not even Marita—would tell me why."

"But she and this Tonio hid you anyway?"

Killian flushed. "Marita and I—well, we hit it off right away."

"So I'd guess," Marne said dryly. "But does she know you're in the army and why you came here?"

"She didn't at first. But I must have talked when I was delirious. Because she and Tonio both knew even though I didn't tell them. And I was lucky they didn't mention it to the sheriff. I heard him tell Marita that Rutter was demanding I be turned over to the CR—and if I turned out to be army, there would be trouble."

He smiled faintly. "But Marita said that I was only a drifting cowhand and she made the old man accept the story. That's when she and Tonio decided I'd have to leave. They knew why I came here—and they approved, as long as I didn't get any natives involved in my fight. That's why they've helped. But they're a frightened people."

"Doncaster's frightened too," Marne murmured. "Or he wouldn't have had Rutter make all that fuss about one man coming into the country. Especially when he couldn't know then you were army."

They reached the shoulder of rock. Marne climbed onto it and used his field glasses to look back. Killian said, "Tonio took me to a place west of the CR and hid me. It's pretty safe, with water and game and a half cave to keep off the weather. There are two well concealed trails leading to it. So until today I came and went as I pleased, using the camp as a base while I tried to find out exactly what's happening at the ranch."

Marne caught movement some distance away. He lowered the glasses. "They're up on this flat," he said. "We haven't got much time. Tell me what you learned."

"Nothing definite," Killian admitted. "In a way, I learned more from Marita and Tonio. But I know this much—that ranch is Doncaster's headquarters, all right. And something is about to happen. He disappeared until yesterday, and then things started moving."

Marne said impatiently, "Give me details."

"Rutter came here over a year ago. He claims to be running a big spread—and he helped himself to it, by the way —but he's only running about fifty head of scrub stock. And for the job he has over two dozen of the toughest looking cowhands I ever saw. Most of them are veterans from the war. You can see that by the way they handle themselves. Besides all those men, Rutter built a half dozen huge barns. They aren't well made but they're well enough guarded. I never did get a look inside one."

"That's where he'll have the wagons with the guns and ammunition," Marne said. "Did you see any wagons coming in?"

"No, but I saw plenty of sign. And there's a yardful of big freighters, being greased and painted and patched up."

Marne swore softly. "But you don't know how much ammunition or how many guns or what kind of supplies Doncaster has?"

"No, sir."

"While we're here, the name is Curt," Marne said gruffly. He added, "Only we won't be here long. We need more information, but this might be enough to help the Colonel." He climbed down from the rock. "I came up this way from the south. You can go back over the trail easier. So leave me a little food and my warbag and get moving. Make the Fort as fast as you can push the horse, and report."

"And you?"

Marne said, "They haven't seen me yet. And if they do, they won't know me. I'm going to try to find out exactly how much Doncaster has to use against us."

Killian said softly, "I was caught today. And I heard the yell, 'army man!' go up. I suspect Carnap had a look at me. And *he* would recognize you."

"I'll try to keep away from Carnap. Besides, I looked like this when I took him in. Once I shave, he won't know me."

"Damn it, sir—Curt. I know this country. I have my hideout. I can stay and . . ."

"And be recognized and shot," Marne said. "I know the country too, remember." He saw the expression on Killian's face and added more gently, "Is it this Marita?"

"We got to know one another pretty well," Killian confessed.

27

"After it's over, you can come back and ask her father for her hand," Marne said dryly.

"He died last year," Killian said. "She runs the inn now." He scowled. "It wasn't because of Marita I thought I should stay. I—"

"If you don't get moving, we'll both stay," Marne snapped. "Permanently. They're getting close! If you aren't over the hump in the rock soon, they'll spot you. Now ride."

Killian made a mock salute and started the dun forward. Marne swore as Killian suddenly swung the animal to his right and raced it out of sight behind a screen of trees. Marne could hear him working northerly, toward the oncoming riders. The sounds faded briefly; then a swirl of noise rose from less than a hundred rods north of Marne's position.

A gun hammered on the thin, cool air. A man shouted in surprise. Horses made wild crashing sounds through the scrub timber. A second gun crashed. A whining voice cried, "He stole my horse! That army joker stole my horse!"

A moment after the sound died, Killian burst through the trees. He was riding the dun and leading a sturdy looking chestnut with a big CR branded on its hip. With a grin of pure deviltry, he tossed the dun's reins to Marne, leaped out of the saddle and onto the chestnut, and swung the horse in the direction he had come.

Marne said savagely, "Lieutenant! I gave an order!"

"I just remembered that you're on leave," Killian said in a low voice. "You know the way back across the big rock, and I know country here. You go and I'll stay."

He flipped his hand and disappeared. Marne stared after him, not knowing whether to laugh or swear.

A deep voice boomed out, "Spread out. Find that man!"

Then, "There he goes. He's heading for the trail down to the valley!" A rifle spat, harsh and sharp. An exultant voice cried, "I winged him!"

The deep voice began to issue commands: "Fitz, go after him. If he gets down the trail first, let him ride. We can pick him up later. Just stay at the head of the trail and keep an eye out for the other one. Tink, you and Smitty get back to the ranch and pick up an extra horse. Then go relieve the men on the west trail."

Marne could see the pattern of the hunt forming. Rutter, or Doncaster, if he was the one giving the orders, was posting men at both of the possible ways out of this trap. Killian didn't concern them at the moment. They had him trapped in the valley, still unable to get away. It was Marne they were concerned with. And, he guessed, Rutter and Doncaster would comb this small area for him with guns ready.

He glanced back at the rock shoulder. He could risk trying to cross it, but the odds were against him. If they rode into sight within the next thirty minutes, they'd find him out in the open, a perfect target.

But he had nowhere else to go. In a few minutes, Rutter and Doncaster would be closing in on him. He remained motionless, sorting out in his mind what he had to do. He rejected the idea of riding for the Colonel. He had too little evidence to offer to make the Colonel risk Washington's anger by sending troops out. No, before he could get any action, Marne knew he would have to get more information—amounts of guns and ammunition, approximate numbers of men, Doncaster's general plan of action, even his starting date.

And then there was Tim Killian. If that man's cry had meant anything, he was trying to hide with a bullet in him. "Winged," the CR man had said. Shot in the shoulder or the arm most likely, Marne judged. For Killian's sake and for his own peace of mind, he would have to find the Lieutenant as quickly as possible.

But the only way to get down into the valley was to go out of the mountains and back in again. And the only way to go out from here was back the way he had come.

Marne climbed into the saddle and headed the dun for the big rock. Once he glanced back and saw nothing. Then he started across the great sweep of worn granite. For the next twenty to thirty minutes, he would be a target no rifleman could miss.

V

MARNE HEARD the riders nearing the rock just as he pulled the dun out of sight on the far side. He let the horse rest while he worked back on his belly to a position where he could use his field glasses.

He watched Doncaster and Rutter mill their horses before the rock. The last yards of ground in front of it were flint hard and, Marne knew, had taken no sign. He grinned as he guessed their bewilderment. Then Rutter straightened and pointed across the rock. Doncaster studied it for some time, shook his head, and swung away. Marne relaxed as they rode out of sight. As far as they knew, he was still somewhere up on that bench.

He returned to the dun and started leading it through the quickening dusk. "We'll go down to the first spring and camp," he said conversationally. "Then tomorrow we'll take the easy trail up."

That would be the first real test. He was sure that none of the men had seen him today, and even if they had it would have been no more than a brief glimpse. He planned to shave off the beard that covered him from cheeks to chin and to change from the roustabout clothes he wore to a puncher's outfit. The main risk then would be if Carnap was here, guarding the trail. Marne was sure that it had been Carnap who had recognized Killian as an army man. There was no other possible explanation.

Sunset the following evening found him pushing through the notch that marked the pass from Mexico into the United States. Each mile had brought more and more surprise to Marne as he saw the way in which the old trail, fit only for mules when he had crossed by it two years before, had been readied for freight wagons. When Doncaster did a job, he did it thoroughly, Marne had to admit.

He stopped at the top of the pass to rest the dun and to survey the country ahead. The timber was thick here and it carpeted the sloping land heavily for some miles down to a wide meadow. It was, Marne recalled, at the near edge of that meadow that the cut-off trail from the eastern bench came in. And there Doncaster's men would be camped, situated so they could watch both trails at the same time.

Beyond the meadow, as Marne remembered it, the trail dropped down to a Y, one branch running down into the valley where the CR would be located now, the other angling a little eastward and on down to the tiny settlement of Arroyo Verde. It was there, at the inn, that he hoped to be for supper tonight.

He started the dun down a series of switchbacks that kinked through the heavy timber. At the bottom of a steep slope the road leveled out and ran straight through a tunnel of trees toward the meadow. The light was failing now, and when two riders appeared out of the timber near the edge of the meadow, Marne was barely able to recognize Tink and Smitty from yesterday. Tink would be the tall, dish-faced one, Smitty the stocky rider with the bandaged hand.

They blocked the trail with their horses. Tink had a carbine out, the barrel resting on his saddlebow, the muzzle aimed at Marne. Smitty held a handgun hanging alongside his leg.

"You, there. Rein up," Tink called. "Where do you think you're going?"

Marne stopped the dun and sat with his hands cupped over the saddlehorn, the reins loose in his fingers.

"That's my business," he said flatly.

"This is private property."

Marne jerked his head toward the south. "I was told back there in the desert that this is an old Indian trail. And the map says this side of the pass belongs to the United States. You might claim the land, friend, but you can't claim the trail."

Tink leaned forward. "This whole country belongs to the CR ranch, mister. Trail and all." He straightened up. "And we don't like strangers nosing around. You want fresh beef, go buy your own."

Marne stifled a desire to laugh. So this was Rutter's excuse for blocking the trails with guards—he claimed to be wary of rustlers.

"Buying myself some beef is just what I had in mind," he said in a pleasant tone. "A nice thick steak. I hear there's a town ahead. Now put that gun away and move aside. I'm tired and hungry."

"He don't hear good this high in the hills," Tink commented. "Smitty, you go clean his ears for him."

Smitty swung his horse into the trees. Marne could hear him riding to get behind him on the trail, putting him in a squeeze between two guns. If he was going to make a move, now would have to be the time.

Carefully, Marne slid his feet back until only his toes were touching the edge of his stirrups. He began to turn, as if reaching for his coat lashed to his warbag.

"Hold it!" Smitty was still riding through the trees. Tink said again, "Hold it, mister!"

Marne turned back. At the same time he lifted himself from the saddle. He kicked against the edges of his stirrups, sending himself cascading off the dun's right shoulder. He landed rolling and dived into the darkness under the nearest trees.

Tink's gun shattered the night. Marne felt the whip of the bullet slash brush against his leg. Then he was on his feet and working his way deeper into darkness and momentary safety.

Tink fired again. Smitty yelled. "I'm back here. And you know what the boss said. He wants that joker we ran into yesterday brought in alive. This could be him."

"Don't be a damn fool," Tink retorted. "That one's down in the valley looking for Killian. How could he have got away to come down this trail? I say, get him!"

Smitty's horse crashed through the brush. The noises stopped, indicating he had reached the trail. Suddenly the night was alive with guns as both men poured lead into the forest. Marne pressed himself behind a thick-boled pine and listened to the whispers of death around him. For the moment he was safe. But the immediate future was another problem.

Tink's voice came clearly as gunfire ceased, and his words echoed Marne's thoughts. "We're wasting lead. And he ain't going far. We got his horse and all his gear. All we got to do is sit and wait until the night air freezes him out of there."

Marne stared at the thick darkness. Tink was right, he realized. This high country could get bitterly cold on a clear night such as this. He could not see well enough to try to slip by them. He dared not build a fire. That would be the same as asking for a bullet.

He had no choice but to make another play, Marne knew. Carefully he slipped through the trees, angling toward the lighter area that marked the trail. He shivered as cold fingers of air rolled off the high peaks and probed through his shirt. He began to think he had been foolish, deliberately walking into their trap this way. But experience had taught him that boldness was often the way to beat long odds.

He had hoped they would take him for what he seemed—a drifter—and let him ride on to Arroyo Verde. They had taken him for a drifter, all right, but apparently Rutter's policy was not to let anyone but his own crew into the Diablos, not even to ride on through them.

Marne reached the edge of the trees. He stepped onto the trail, drawing his .44 as he moved. He glanced to the south. Tink and Smitty were sitting their horses near the dun, a good twenty feet away.

Marne said with soft mockery, "You're looking in the wrong place, gents." His voice sharpened. "Drop those guns—fast!"

Tink turned and raised his rifle. Marne fired, sending lead whistling by the brim of Tink's hat. Smitty dropped his rifle and lifted both hands high. Slowly, Tink followed suit.

Marne said, "Now back your horses away from mine. Keep moving. That's far enough. Hold it there!"

Tink started to wheel for the trees. Marne's gun spat fire into the darkness. The bullet whipped dirt by Tink's horse's hoofs. The animal reared up. Tink jerked it down and sat sullenly.

' Marne walked up to the dun and climbed into the saddle without taking his gun or his eyes off either man.

"This ain't going to get you nothing but trouble," Tink said. "This is CR country. If you're smart, you'll make it easy on yourself and ride out of here quick."

"I'm a peaceable man," Marne said. "But you kind of make me forget that." His voice sharpened to a tone of command again. "Now pull your hardware off your hips and let it hit the ground."

Two handguns dropped through the darkness onto the trail. Marne pulled the dun to one side. "Now ride past me—slow and easy."

He wanted to laugh at Tink's sour expression as the dish-faced man moved slowly by him. Smitty only looked frightened. He wasn't much, Marne decided. Of the two, Tink would be the one to watch. There was alertness and intelligence in his gaze. Despite his remark that Marne couldn't be the one they were looking for, his slow, steady look suggested that he might be having second thoughts.

Once they were by, Marne halted them. Then he gathered up the guns and settled in the saddle. "Now ride for Arroyo Verde. And don't forget that I'm behind you with all the guns."

They rode in silence, out of the trees, across the broad meadow, and down to the edge of the bench below. The trail forked here and Tink reined toward the left branch.

Marne said quietly, "The map shows that the trail to town is the one going straight ahead. Keep on it!"

"You ain't going to get far hoorawing us this way," Tink said.

"Save your breath for the law," Marne snapped.

"The law!" Tink guffawed suddenly, filling the darkness with heavy laughter. "You're taking us to the sheriff in Arroyo Verde?"

"That's right," Marne said. "Now move on."

He wondered at the cause of Tink's amusement. Sheriff

Potrero's law had not been laughed at two years ago. As Marne remembered, he ruled these mountains almost as a benevolent despot. Then Marne recalled Tim Killian's story.

He would soon know the answer. The town of Arroyo Verde could be made out by the cluster of lights gleaming up from a cup of darkness below. That black bulk would be the cathedral, Marne remembered. It was set against the hillside with its front facing the plaza. On the right of the church would be the livery barn, the city office with its two jail cells, and the barber shop. Opposite the cathedral but set a short distance back of the plaza was the Posada Farrel. Marne felt a twinge of regret for Tim Farrel. The handsome, grinning Irishman and his striking Spanish wife stood out clearly in his memory. Their deaths must have left a hole in many lives.

Marne tried to remember their daughter, Marita. He decided she must have been the child away at school in St. Louis. But not too much of a child if she was old enough to attract Tim Killian.

They reached the plaza. At this hour it was quiet, with only the jail office and the posada showing lights. Marne ordered Tink and Smitty to tie their horses in front of the jail. "I'll see to your horses," he added.

Tink laughed. "Don't trouble yourself. We'll do that little chore ourselves—after we take care of you."

Marne dropped out of the saddle. "Get inside," he ordered coldly. He frowned as Tink swaggered into the building as if he might be the sheriff. Smitty followed less confidently.

The jail office was small, with barely enough room for the desk, two chairs, and the locked gunrack on the wall. Both the office and the two jail cells were empty.

Tink turned with a mocking grin. "You want us to wait while you go find the law, friend?"

Marne opened the desk drawer and lifted out a ring of keys. "That's right," he said. Unlocking the door to the first cell, he motioned with his gun. "Inside."

Tink's grin faded. "Now listen . . ."

THE HOLDOUT IN THE DIABLOS

"Inside!"

Tink and Smitty stepped into the cell. Marne slammed the door shut. Tink glared from between the bars. "You ain't the law. You can't do this."

"It's done," Marne said quietly. Returning the keys to the desk, he walked outside, shutting the office door behind him.

He crossed the small plaza and entered the lobby of the posada. Open doors on the left showed him the lighted cantina with a half dozen local men grouped around the deal tables and two lined up at the bar. To the right was the dark, deserted dining room, and straight ahead stairs ran to the sleeping rooms on the second floor. To one side of the staircase a corner with a door behind it was cut off by a counter. As Marne approached, a girl opened the door and stepped up to the counter.

This must be Farrel's daughter, Marne decided. She was almost as tall as he remembered her father being. She was slender as well, but with a woman's rounded slenderness. She carried herself with her head held high, reminding him of the Spanish women he had known. But where those women's hair and eyes had been glowing black, this girl's hair was the color of a chestnut's glossy coat and her eyes were a deep smoky gray, only a shade darker than Marne's own. She studied him in surprise.

She said nothing and after a moment Marne spoke up. "I'm looking for the sheriff, miss."

A shadow of fear brushed away the surprise in her expression. "Who are you? How did you get into these mountains?" Her voice was deep and musical, taking some of the sharpness from her words.

"I drifted in over Diablo Pass," Marne said. He saw the fear strengthen on her face and he tried to brush it aside with a light tone. "If you're wondering about the pair that stand guard up there, don't bother. I just finished locking them in a cell. That's why I want the sheriff. I've brought him some business."

To Marne's surprise, a glint of panic flared in her eyes. "*Madre de Diós!*" she whispered.

36

Suddenly she thrust herself forward, anger blazing now where there had been fear before. "Who are you?" she cried. "Are you one of their men—trying to trick us again? Why can't you leave us alone?"

Marne stared uncomprehendingly at her. Then she moved again, this time darting to one end of the counter. Her hand snaked down swiftly. When she stepped back, she held a gun. She aimed it deliberately at Marne, and the expression on her face cried out her desire to kill him.

VI

MARNE STOOD very still, watching carefully the hysteria in Marita Farrel's eyes. She was too close for him to have much chance of dropping out of the path of a bullet. Yet she was too far away for him to reach out and snatch the gun before she could fire it. His one hope would be to distract her long enough to move within reaching distance of her.

He said carefully, "If you mean, am I one of Rutter's men—no. I'm a friend of . . ." He let his voice break off. "That door behind you, Miss Farrel!"

He spoke sharply, trying to jar her. It was a calculated risk, he knew. His maneuver could make her shoot first and look afterwards. But she turned her head toward the door. Marne stepped quickly forward and plucked the gun from her hand. He laid it on the counter top, covering it with his palm.

She looked at him with contempt. "I wouldn't have shot you—even though I wanted to."

Marne's lips tipped up in a faint grin. "I feel more comfortable this way, Miss Farrel."

His second use of her name caught her attention. "I'm sure you know all about me and about everyone here. I'm sure that Rutter or Doncaster told you everything you needed to know to—to trick us."

The anger was rising in her again, and Marne said quickly, "I'm not trying to trick anybody. I'm here because this is the only hotel in three days' ride. And I'm looking for the sheriff because some crazy cowhands tried to stop me from getting this far."

She shook her head stiffly, her expression stubborn. He could only guess at what she might have said or done next. The door behind her opened. A man, some two or three years younger than she, stepped up beside her. Marne had a vague memory of having seen him before—the slender whipcord build, the hot dark eyes, the black hair curling off a broad forehead. His scowl slashed at Marne.

"What is happening here?" he demanded in strongly accented English.

Marita spoke to him rapidly in Spanish. Marne slipped on a blank expression as he listened. It was an old trick of his, to pretend not to understand the language; and more than once it had gained him valuable information. Now he heard Marita tell the story exactly as it had happened. She added, "I think this man is one of Rutter's spies. Have you seen him before, Tonio?"

So this was Tonio, who had helped Tim Killian. Marne was not surprised. The boy and the girl bore a partial resemblance, about what he had expected between cousins.

Tonio frowned. "The last time I was the one who thought someone was a spy," he said, still in Spanish. "But we know I was wrong. It might be the same with this man." He stopped and looked thoughtfully at Marne, his lower lip pushed well out.

"Señor, tell me. You started to say to the señorita here that you were a friend of someone."

Marne leaned forward and spoke softly. "Tim Killian," he said.

Marita's cheeks flushed and her eyes flamed at him. Tonio's scowl deepened. "You are either a liar or an army man then!"

Marne remembered Killian's warning about the fear here of anyone representing the United States. He said quickly,

"I was on duty with him a while back. But I'm not any longer." It was, he thought with a touch of sour humor, in one sense the truth. As the Colonel had pointed out, Marne was on his own as long as his leave lasted.

Marita spoke. "What are you doing here? What do you want with us?"

"Help," Marne said frankly. He saw that he had caught their interest and quickly he sketched what had happened yesterday. He made no effort to explain his reasons for having come into the Diablos.

"If this is true," Marita said in Spanish, "then Tim is hurt He needs someone to help him."

"If it is true," Tonio said, and now the suspicion against Marne seemed to come more strongly from him. "How do we know this one is not just trying to find out Tim's hiding place?"

"Perhaps grandfather heard of some shooting yesterday—or one of the vaqueros," she suggested. Marne felt a lessening of her violent dislike when she looked at him now.

"I have heard nothing," Tonio said. "I have been in the cantina all day. And last night. I would have heard."

"Maybe," she said. "I think before we do anything, we should ask the *abuelo*."

Tonio looked as if he wanted to argue. Then he shrugged. *Sí, Marita. Tú eres la mera gallina.*

Marne swallowed a desire to laugh at Marita's expression. She was obviously embarrassed and she glanced his way as if to reassure herself that he understood no Spanish. Marne scarcely blamed her for being embarrassed. If Tonio's remark hadn't been tinged with affection, it could have been taken as an insult. In this part of the border country, a *mero gallo* was slang for "big boss," although it meant only a "mere chicken" or "pure rooster." By making the words feminine, Tonio had called Marita the chief hen in the chicken house.

"I'll get the *abuelo*," Tonio said. He walked around the counter and toward the door leading into the cantina.

"Tonio has gone for the sheriff, my grandfather," Marita said to Marne.

He managed to show pleasure. "Then maybe we can get the trouble over with and I can get some supper and go to bed."

Before she could answer, footsteps turned Marne around. He recognized the lean, spare old man coming toward him as Manuel Potrero. He looked as Marne remembered him, but older than a gap of two short years could explain. His silver hair had lost its life and turned a dull, dying white. The spring was gone from his step and the glint from his dark eyes. And the wrinkles seemed burned more deeply into his tanned features.

"Yes, *señor?*" He showed no sign of recognition as he looked at Marne. A beard made a lot of difference, Marne thought. That and two years.

Marne told his story about bringing in Tink and Smitty. Marita translated into Spanish as if wanting to make sure that her grandfather understood.

The sheriff looked unhappy as the story unfolded. When it was finished, he said, "If this is true, we may have trouble because of this man. It is not a joke Rutter will forgive easily. If it is not true, we must take care. This one may be another trick to bring us grief and let them remind us of their power." As Tonio had, he spoke Spanish to Marita. Then he stared at Marne worriedly, obviously wondering how much he had understood.

Marita said quickly, "Do not worry. He does not speak our language." Without looking at Marne, she added slowly, in a clear voice, *"No es verdad, hijo de un asno?"*

Marne fought down a desire to burst out laughing. It wasn't every day that a strikingly attractive woman called him the son of a jackass.

The old man said sharply, *"Basta!* That is enough foolishness. Until we are certain, we must accept this man as our guest." He turned to Marne and spoke in English. "Let us go to the jail."

On their way across the plaza, the sheriff said, "Why did you do this? Do you wish to make troubles for the CR ranch?"

"I never heard of the CR ranch and I never saw those two

men until I came into the Diablos," Marne answered truth-fully. "But they were waving guns on a public road. I took them for a pair of hardcases trying to rob me."

"And you will wish to prefer charges?" The old man sounded worried. Marne shook his head in wonderment. This was hardly the same Manuel Potrero he had seen two years ago. Then the man had been alive, vital, and he had kept order in the Diablos with a powerful, if smooth, hand.

They entered the jail office. Tink was standing at the door to his cell. He scowled. "Come on, old man, open up. Let us out of here. And put this joker inside. Maybe a few days in jail will teach him who's boss in these parts."

The sheriff picked up his keys. Then with sudden decision he dropped them back to the desk. "I am still the law here!" he said stiffly. "This man has charged you with molesting him on a public road. I will hear your story."

Tink curbed his anger with an obvious effort. "Molested him, hell! Me and Smitty was up by the meadow as peace-able as a couple of cows in a hayfield when this joker rode down from the pass. Well, we hid to see what he was up to. And so help me, he headed straight into the meadow, picked himself out a prime young piece of CR beef and got ready to kill himself some dinner. Naturally we pulled our guns. But he got the jump on us and hauled us in here."

"He's lying," Marne said quietly.

"Ask Smitty," Tink said mockingly. "Sheriff, whose word you taking—ours or the drifter's?"

Potrero looked uncomfortable. But he said coldly, "There are no cattle in the meadow. I was there earlier today. There has not been a cow on that grass since in the spring."

"It was getting dark," Tink said in the same mocking tone. "Maybe there wasn't a steer. Maybe it was a shadow. But we sure thought he was rustling."

The sheriff looked at Marne. "I do not believe them. But I cannot hold them on your word alone. If you had a wit-ness . . ."

They have him scared, Marne thought wonderingly. He looked more closely at the old man. Not scared for himself.

Marne could not imagine Potrero afraid of anything. But for some reason he was frightened of what Tink and Smitty represented. And that fear had turned his self pride to ashes.

Tink said, "Let us out, old man. The boss'll be in the cantina by now, and I want to talk to him."

He turned bleak, hate-filled eyes on Marne. "I want to ask him what to do about this joker."

VII

WHILE THE sheriff was releasing Tink and Smitty, Marne left to stable his dun and then to return to the *posada* for a room. Marita was behind the counter and when he asked for a bed, she turned the register book toward him without a comment.

He scrawled "Curtis Marne" on the page but deliberately left the column for his place of residence blank. Marita looked at him with lifted eyebrows.

Marne smiled at her. "Now that I'm not on army duty any more, I don't live much of anyplace," he said. He set the pen back in its glass of shot and took the heavy key she handed him. "Can I get some supper after a while?"

"Tonio will bring you food in the cantina," she answered. As he started away, she called softly, "Señor Marne . . ."

He turned. She seemed hesitant and he stepped closer to her. She said in a low voice, "About Tim Killian—what you said is true?"

"It's true. But I wouldn't tell anyone—not even the sheriff."

She started to nod, caught herself. "Why do you say that?"

"Tim told me that you and Tonio had to hide him, even from the sheriff," Marne said frankly. He watched her expression carefully. "He said that your grandfather was afraid of something—afraid enough to turn him over to this Rutter and his CR crew."

The door behind Marita had opened and Tonio slipped in while Marne talked. The boy said in Spanish to Marita, "The story must be true. How else would he know these things?"

She nodded and her expression grew even more friendly as she looked again at Marne. "Do you know where Tim is now?"

Marne shook his head. "My guess is he headed back for the hiding place Tonio here took him to before. From the noise Rutter and Doncaster were making, I think he got off the bench and down to the valley all right."

"This man Doncaster. You speak as if you know him," Tonio said sharply.

Marne suppressed a sigh. The boy's suspicion was less but it was obviously not all gone. He wondered just what he would have to do to get Tonio's complete trust.

"I saw him yesterday. I heard him talk with Rutter. When I was on duty I heard a lot about him."

Tonio shrugged. He said suddenly, "You are here because you wish Marita or me to take you to where Tim Killian is hiding?"

"Somebody has to get to him," Marne said slowly. "I told you I think he's wounded."

"Do you know why he is in these mountains?" Again the question was sharp.

"He said he was chasing an escaped prisoner from the fort," Marne answered frankly.

"He told you nothing more?"

"Why should he?" Marne demanded. "I happened into the fight. I helped him. That doesn't make his business my business." It was the closest he had come to direct lying and it made him uncomfortable under Tonio's probing gaze.

"We will talk about Tim later," Tonio said abruptly. "Come into the cantina and I will find you some food." He turned and walked away.

Marne went up the stairs to his room. Here he washed the trail dirt off, brushed dust from his clothes and hat, and slipped on a fresh shirt. He went back downstairs and into the cantina.

It was a medium sized room with a cleared space between clusters of round tables and the long bar. Four men, obviously natives of the Diablos, sat at one of the tables. Some distance away Doncaster and Rutter sat by themselves. Tink and Smitty were at the next table, with Tink's chair swiveled around so that he could talk to Rutter. Tonio was the only other person in the room. He worked desultorily at wiping the bar top.

Marne chucked to himself as Tink stabbed a finger in his direction. He saw Rutter turn and measure him with a cold, dark glance. Doncaster looked too, but his gaze had more meaning to it. Rutter showed little more than irritation and dislike; Doncaster was obviously suspicious of Marne, and curious as well.

Marne returned their looks with no expression and then took a seat at the table nearest the bar. In a moment Tonio came up to him. "This late all I can bring you is meat tacos," he said.

"That'll do fine," Marne said. "And some beer to wash it down with."

He turned his attention briefly to Tonio. At his entry, the boy had looked worriedly from Rutter to him. Not, Marne guessed, because he feared a fight, but because he feared his suspicions might be right after all—that Marne was one of the CR outfit. Now, Marne noticed with sour amusement, Tonio kept watching as he worked.

When Tonio set down a plate of tacos and a heavy mug of beer, Marne said softly, "The one called Tink seems to be working himself up to a fight. How many of the local men can I count on against the CR?"

"None of them," Tonio said flatly. "I would not fight, Señor Marne. It will gain you nothing."

"You never know," Marne murmured. He turned to his food.

He was hungry and he ate quickly. He was wiping his plate with a last scrap of tortilla when Tink came out of his chair and swaggered to Marne's table. He leaned forward, placing both hands flat on the tabletop. His expression was insolent.

"The boss wants to talk to you."

Marne glanced past Tink's shoulder and looked squarely at Rutter. "If he wants to talk to me, let him get over here and do it."

Tink straightened up in surprise. He seemed to find it hard to believe that a man like Marne—an obvious drifter—would talk this way to a man of Rutter's importance. Marne could see the flush wash over Rutter's face and he grinned mockingly at the anger flaring in Rutter's eyes.

Marne lifted a hand toward Tonio. "Bring me another beer, amigo."

Rutter thrust his head forward. "Bring that joker over here, Tink!"

Marne was out of his chair before Tink's hand was close to his gun butt. He caught Tink by the arm and spun him. At the same time, he knocked Tink's gunhand up and jerked the .44 from its holster. Off balance, Tink staggered to one side. Marne sat back down, the gun in his hand.

"Run your own errands, little man," he said to Rutter.

Rutter was on his feet. Doncaster murmured something to him but he shook his head, as if he was refusing advice. "Listen, stranger, those are my men you've been hoorawing. What are you trying to prove? What are you doing in these parts?"

"That's my business," Marne said shortly.

"What happens in the Diablos is my affair," Rutter answered.

Marne ignored him and glanced toward Tonio. The boy stood indecisively at the end of the bar, the fresh mug of beer in his hand. Marne waved him forward. "All this noise is making me thirsty," he said.

Tonio came toward him. Rutter took an angry step forward and then he rushed at Marne's table. "The devil with your beer!" he cried. His arm swept out, catching Tonio in the chest and sending him crashing backward against the edge of the bar. The mug fell, shattering on the floor. Rutter checked himself a few feet from where Marne sat. "You're coming with me!"

Marne said softly, "That was my beer. Mop up that mess and get me another glass."

Rutter gaped at him. Then anger overwhelmed his surprise. The cords in his neck and jaws stood out tautly. "You're talking to Carl Rutter, drifter. Now, by God, get on your feet and . . ."

Marne glanced toward the other men in the room. The four natives were sitting very quietly, watching but making no moves to interfere. Tink and Smitty were at their table. They weren't interfering either—obviously because Doncaster was holding them quiet. He had one hand lifted toward the pair. At the same time he was watching the scene between Marne and Rutter. His expression was thoughtful.

Marne wondered, Is he trying to tie me to the man who helped Killian yesterday or the man who almost trapped him in Arizona Territory last month? Or, he thought, is Doncaster concerned about Rutter? No general liked to see his seconds in command unable to contain their tempers, Marne knew.

Marne rose. He towered half a head over Rutter, but the other man was heavier with a powerful, thick body and long arms ending in big, solid knuckled hands.

Marne said, "I told you to mop up that mess before I wipe your face in it."

Rutter reached for Marne's shirtfront. Marne sensed the move coming and stepped aside. His hand shot out and down, cutting the edge of his palm across Rutter's wrist. Rutter swore in pain and surprise. He jerked his hand back and drove it, fist clenched, for Marne's face.

Marne leaned away from the blow and flicked hard knuckles against Rutter's nose. Rutter moved back, blinking. Now Marne carried the fight forward. His mouth was flattened in a harsh grin as he knocked Rutter's guard aside and ripped both fists into the heavy body. He felt a layer of fat, but under it was the solidity of heavy muscle.

Rutter stood his ground now and reached to get Marne

in a rib-cracking bear hug. Marne danced back and smashed Rutter again on his fleshy nose. Rutter moved another step back, obviously hurt. Marne battered a fist against his lips and another into the soft flesh beneath his eyes. Rutter was plainly no boxer, and Marne was too fast for his roughhouse swings to reach their mark. He was forced back, grudging step by grudging step until the edge of the bar caught him across the back.

Marne said, "When you ask for a mop, I'll let up, Rutter."

Blood trickled from Rutter's battered mouth. "Go to hell!" He pushed himself forward, hands pawing for Marne. He slammed back against the bar as Marne hit him savagely in the face with two quick fists. Rutter sagged, holding himself up only by hooking his elbows over the bar at his back.

"That's enough!" a sharp voice cracked out.

Marne stepped aside and glanced toward the center of the room. Doncaster stood there, his gun drawn. Beside him, Smitty also had his .44 out. "You've had your fun," Doncaster said. "Now you pay the price. You're riding out with us."

From the bar, Tonio's young voice came clearly. "No, señores." He had a shotgun laid on the bar, his finger lightly on the trigger. "The gun is loaded," he added softly. "The Señor Rutter started the fight. Let him finish it without your help."

Marne saw the expression in Tonio's eyes and realized what this action was costing him. He turned away and watched as Doncaster and Smitty slowly holstered their guns. Doncaster sat down and drummed his fingers softly on the tabletop. "We'll remember this," he said in a deadly soft voice.

"So will he," Marne said. He reached out and caught Rutter's shirtfront. Rutter staggered as Marne pulled him forward. His face was a mask of blood and bruises. One eye was closed. The other was half shut. His nose and mouth looked like two pieces of pulpy red fruit. Marne pushed him toward Doncaster. "Take him home," he ordered.

Rutter caught his balance suddenly. He turned and rushed wildly at Marne. The element of surprise was his and his flailing fist caught Marne's temple. Marne crashed sideways, knocking over a chair. He skidded a half dozen feet across the splintery floor before he could get control of himself. Rutter was rushing him again. He came up against Marne chest to chest and started swinging his arms, sending his fists into Marne's body in great sledgehammer blows. Marne felt his wind go under the sudden onslaught, and for a moment he could only hang on and fight for strength.

"*Basta!*" an authoritative voice snapped from the doorway. Rutter checked a swing. Marne stepped to one side and turned. The sheriff stood in the entry, his gun in his hand. His eyes swept coldly over the room.

"Get out, all of you. There will be no fighting in Arroyo Verde."

Rutter made a thick laughing sound. Marne heard his bootsoles scrape on the floor and he turned barely in time to see the blur of Rutter's body charging down on him.

Marne dropped into a crouch and swung a shoulder. He drove upward with a powerful thrust of his legs just as Rutter reached him. The point of his shoulder drove into Rutter's middle. Marne followed his charge, keeping Rutter staggering backwards. He stopped suddenly and Rutter crashed into a table and rolled onto the floor.

"Enough!" the sheriff repeated. "One more move and you go to jail."

"Him or me?" Marne asked quietly.

Rutter got to his feet. He wiped his sleeve across his face, smearing blood and sweat. "Look, old man, I told you before who's boss in these mountains. Me! I'm taking this drifter with me. You go play your games someplace else."

Marne stood aside and watched with interest as Rutter and the sheriff faced one another. He saw indecision touch the old man's features. Then anger crowded it out as Rutter cried, "And I'm taking that fool kid too. He needs a lesson!"

"That boy is my grandson," Potrero whispered.

"He threw that shotgun on my men!"

Marne glanced toward Tonio. He still held the shotgun but now his expression was one of fear. Marne saw why.

Doncaster had not risen from his chair but he had drawn his gun. It was pointed at the sheriff. It was clear enough that he could shoot as fast as Tonio could.

Marne said, "Put up your guns," to Tonio and the sheriff. "I want no killings on my account."

Both Tonio and Potrero hesitated. Doncaster said sharply, "Do what he says, old man. You, too, chiquito."

Resentment at the Spanish term for "little one" brought a flush to Tonio's cheeks. But the sharply spoken command seemed to get through to both him and the sheriff. The shotgun disappeared. Potrero's gun went back in its holster. Now Doncaster was the only man armed and ready.

He said to Potrero, "You've been told what to do with strangers if any show up here. Why didn't you lock this one up and hold him for us?"

Potrero stared at him from cold, hate-glutted eyes. But he made no answer. After a moment, he walked to the nearest table and dropped heavily onto a chair. He sat motionless, his face white with the pallor of death.

Marne wondered what the next move would be. He could reach for his own gun but not without risking a shot from Doncaster. Then he heard a footstep behind him. He turned to see Rutter coming up, gun in hand. He stood helplessly while Rutter took his .44 from its holster.

Rutter motioned to Tink and Smitty. "Come over here, boys. In a minute I'll need you to hold this joker on his feet." His battered lips skinned back from his teeth. "Now it's my turn to pound some meat!"

VIII

Marne had seen a crew work over a victim this way in tavern fights and in barracks brawls. If there were three men, two would hold and one would swing at the helpless target until his arms grew tired. Once Marne had seen a man die from just such a beating.

He watched silently as Tink and Smitty swaggered up and took their positions, one on either side of him. Their hands bit into his arms and they jerked together, slamming him roughly back so that the rounded edge of the bar jarred against his spine.

Now it was Rutter's turn. His lips twisted into a grin, he came around to stand squarely in front of Marne. He holstered his .44 and drew back his massive right fist.

He had one chance in a thousand of living through this, Marne knew. The glint in Rutter's eyes was murderous. He had taken a humiliating beating, not only in front of his men but in front of Doncaster as well. It would take more than just whipping Marne to satisfy his scarred pride.

Carefully, Marne lifted his right leg. His eyes were fixed on Rutter's poised right fist. At the instant Rutter lunged forward, throwing his weight behind the driving surge of his arm, Marne shot his foot out and down, raking his bootsole savagely down Rutter's shin. In a continuation of the same motion, Marne leaned to one side and swung his left shoulder with all the force he could manage. He pulled Smitty out of position, bringing him stumbling around to take the full force of Rutter's fist. Smitty's shout was drowned in Rutter's curse of pain.

As Smitty's grip slipped from his arm, Marne brought his hand around and caught Tink by the shirtfront. He jerked and Tink came swinging around the way Smitty had a moment before. But now Rutter had untangled himself from the short man and was backpedaling, pawing for his gun.

Marne drove a vicious fist against the back of Tink's ear, sending the dish-faced man staggering forward into Rutter. Tink slid off Rutter's chest and flopped to the floor. The force of his stumbling body had Rutter off balance, unable to get a solid grip on his gun, and he kept pawing for it and cursing in a thick, crazy voice.

Marne rushed him. Rutter managed a roundhouse swing that made Marne feel as if his ribs had been driven through his body. Then he had one hand on his own .44 and he pulled it out of Rutter's belt, where the man had rammed it earlier.

At the same time Marne gave Rutter a solid push that sent him on backwards, staggering toward Doncaster's table.

Marne had had a quick glimpse of Doncaster coming to his feet. From the man's expression, he knew that Doncaster was no longer being entertained by the sight of his second in command being manhandled. It was quickly becoming a matter of prestige, of maintaining the control he somehow had managed to impose on people like Sheriff Potrero. And Doncaster was raising his gun—to rid himself of Marne once and for all.

He swore and tried to sidestep Rutter stumbling backwards. Rutter hit the table and smashed it to the floor. He lay in the ruins, cursing. Doncaster was well to one side now but he brought his gun only halfway up when he stopped abruptly and let it fall again.

Marne stood back by the bar, Tink and Smitty lay soggily unconscious in front of him. He had his gun hip high, the muzzle trained unwaveringly on Doncaster.

"They're yours, if you ache to arrest them, sheriff," Marne said. He was grinning, and the light in his smoky eyes was one of sheer pleasure. The air was still filled with tension, with the feeling that it might explode at any instant, and the sensations ran through him like no liquor could.

Doncaster swiveled his head toward Potrero, who had not moved since taking his chair. "This was just a friendly fight, old man. Let's leave it that way."

Potrero said tiredly, "Do you have a charge to bring, señor?"

"No charge," Marne said. "But since it was just a friendly fight, the CR here won't mind my riding on through these mountains tomorrow."

A shadow crossed Potrero's features. He glanced at Doncaster. Doncaster shrugged. "I was under the impression you were looking for work instead of just drifting. If so, I can offer you a job on the CR."

"Doing what?" Marne asked softly.

"Why, punching cattle, driving a wagon, odds and ends of ranch work." He bent down and hauled Rutter to his feet.

51

He said something too low for Marne to hear and Rutter moved forward and began working to bring Tink and Smitty back to life.

Doncaster kept his eyes on Marne. "If you're interested, come out to the ranch tomorrow. Anybody here can tell you the way."

Silently Marne cursed him. He had originally forced the fight in an effort to get Tonio and Marita to believe more firmly in his story, to lose their suspicions that he might be one of Rutter's men. And considering Tonio's actions, he had apparently succeeded. But talk such as this from Doncaster could only bring that suspicion back, particularly to Tonio, who stood listening from his position behind the bar.

"I might do that," Marne said shortly. He turned away and nodded at Tonio. "I could do with a glass of whiskey about now."

Silently the boy poured him a shot. Marne took it down quickly, wanting the heat of it. He poured a second glass and sipped this one slowly. He remained silent as Ritter and Doncaster helped Smitty and Tink out of the bar. Soon the sound of their horses hammering out of town could be heard. The sounds faded and the thick silence in the cantina suddenly shattered.

The four men at the one table began chattering to one another in Spanish. Potrero rose and came to stand near Marne. Tonio moved opposite Marne, leaning forward so that he was very close.

"You started that fight," Tonio said. "Why, Señor Marne?"

"Rutter was trying to push me," Marne said. "I don't take to being pushed."

"Will you go to the rancho tomorrow?" Potrero demanded suddenly.

Marne turned his head and smiled thinly. "And get myself beaten to death? Or shot—if I'm lucky? No thanks."

"Do you think they will let you ride freely from the Diablos?"

Marne said frankly, "I don't even think they want to let me live through the night. More than likely, they'd have me disappear before morning. That way they could claim they knew nothing about what happened to me. If I went to the ranch and disappeared, it would be obvious who caused it."

"You think they care for anyone's opinion, Señor Marne?" Tonio demanded.

"Some," Marne said. "If they didn't, they could have shot me the minute I came down the trail earlier today. Or here tonight."

He emptied his whiskey glass, nodded at the sheriff, and turned away. "I think I'll get some sleep. I'm a little tired after what happened."

They were silent as he walked out of the room and on up the stairs. He shut his door but left it unlocked. Peeling off his shirt, he examined his bruises by lamplight, washed them in cold water, and decided none was bad enough to do more than make him a little stiff and sore. Turning to his warbag, he packed the few things he had removed and then sat down to wait. After a moment, he rose and blew out the lamp.

He could hear sounds coming up from below, of men leaving the cantina, of Tonio or Marita stirring around as whoever it was locked up for the night. Then he caught the soft footfalls coming up the stairs. When a hand touched the latch on his door, Marne moved softly to the window and raised the shade. Moonlight flooded in, making a path from sill to the doorway. He stood in shadow, his hand on his gun.

The door swung quietly open. Moonlight outlined Marita's graceful form as she came into the room. Marne stepped out where she could see him.

"Señor Marne, you must leave quickly!" she whispered. "Tonio told me what happened. And it is true, what you said in the cantina. Those men will come and try to kill you tonight."

"Leave for where?" he asked. "I can't ride the trails if they're guarded." He shook his head. "Besides, I told you Tim Killian is wounded. He's got to be seen to first thing."

"Tonio and I will take care of that. You must go."

"Go where?" Marne said again.

"There is a place you can hide. Tonio will show it to you."

Marne said steadily, "I know how to get out of these mountains without taking one of the guarded trails. If Killian can travel, I can slip him away from here. All I need is about an hour's start on the CR."

Tonio had apparently come upstairs too quietly for Marne to hear him. He spoke suddenly from the doorway. "Why are you so insistent that we take you to Killian, Señor Marne?"

"I told you," Marne said. "We were friends when I was on duty at the fort. I helped him out yesterday. Why do you think I came back into these mountains if I didn't want to help him?"

"You could have come to have us show you where he is hiding. You could be doing this for Rutter and for Doncaster."

"Can't you get that foolishness out of your head?" Marne demanded. "If I'd wanted him killed, why would I have helped him yesterday?"

"To get in with us," Tonio said. "To be—to be where you could learn things about us."

"Don't be an idiot," Marne said roughly. "You weren't even around yesterday to see what I did to help Killian. Why would I go to all that trouble before I ever heard of you two?"

He stepped forward. "I know you're having trouble. I can see that your grandfather is more of a man than he acted tonight. I don't know what kind of power the CR holds over him—and over everyone else here—but I'd like to know. I'd like to help."

"Tonio," Marita whispered, "why do you refuse to believe the Señor Marne? Did you not see for yourself the fight . . . ?"

She had spoken to him in Spanish, and he answered her in the same language: "I must be sure. If we take him to Tim Killian and we are wrong, you know what can happen. If we help him and he is not one of theirs, you know what they will do. We must be sure!"

"We cannot let them drive us like animals forever!" she cried fiercely. "We must fight sometime. You saw what happened tonight. This man can help us fight!"

THE HOLDOUT IN THE DIABLOS

Footfalls coming purposefully up the stairs cut sharply through the conversation. Marita motioned to the window. "Quickly—take your bag and go out. There is a roof a few feet below you. It is dark there. If this is one of them, perhaps they will not find you. . . ."

Marne caught up his warbag and slipped to the window. He let it fall to the flat roof of a veranda below. Then he lowered himself from the sill by his hands. His toes brushed the roof and he let himself down onto it. He stood pressed against the wall, listening to the sounds from above.

He did not expect it to be Doncaster or any of his men. Rather, he expected the newcomer to be the sheriff—and he had a good idea of Potrero's reason for coming here at this hour.

"Where is the Señor Marne?" he demanded in a clear voice.

"We came to see if he was badly hurt," Marita said. "But we found him gone."

"I think he was afraid and ran away," Tonio said.

"On foot? His horse is still at the livery." The old man's voice sharpened. "Are you hiding him—as you hid that other man?"

"What reason would we have?" Marita's voice became sharp too. "Why do you talk this way to us, *abuelo?* What do you want with the Señor Marne?"

The sheriff's voice was tired, heavy. "I have come to arrest him."

He had guessed right, Marne thought. He shifted his position carefully and continued to listen.

"Arrest him—for what?" the girl demanded.

"Doncaster wants to be sure he is here tomorrow. He will come for Marne and take him to the rancho," the sheriff said.

"To kill him!"

"First, to question him. Doncaster is worried. He cannot understand a man like this Marne. One who fights against odds, and smiles as he does it. I think he is frightened—as men like him are always frightened of the things they do not understand, that they cannot control."

"But after they question him, they will kill him! And you will let this happen. You will help them do this!"

The old man's voice had no life in it. "What else can I do? You know the choice I must make. I am sorry, little one."

He paused and added slowly, "I would kill Marne myself if they ordered me to do so."

IX

DONCASTER PACED the big bare kitchen of the CR ranch house. He stopped and glared at Rutter seated at the table. He watched sourly as Rutter sucked coffee through his battered lips.

"I let you go on tonight to see how far you'd carry things," Doncaster said. "And that temper of yours nearly cost us real trouble. Is that the way you've run things while I've been out setting up the raids?"

"That drifter made a fool out of me!" Rutter snarled. "I had to show those natives what happens to someone who does that to me."

"Is that why you let that army man get away from you—to show the natives? Is that why you let a kid like Tonio Potrero make a fool of us all when he slapped that shotgun down on the bar—to show the natives? Is that why you let the drifter beat you half to jelly?"

Doncaster's voice was ripe with scorn, and Rutter winced under the words as if each were a whiplash. He said finally, in a tone of desperation, "Everything's been going good lately. You said as much yourself. All the guns and ammunition are here and most of them loaded. Only a few wagons haven't been shaped up for the trip out. I got us all the men we need . . ."

"You got us one—or maybe two—too many," Doncaster said heavily. "If that army man gets out of the Diablos, where do you think he's going? And after what you did to the drifter, which side is he going to be on? And what happened to the joker who helped Killian yesterday? You claim to know these mountains. But he got away from you."

Doncaster's concern showed in the roughness of his voice. He was usually a man who kept his temper, who thought things through before acting on them, who believed in planning to the final move. When something interfered with his plans, he had taught himself to adjust; but it was not a thing he relished, and when he could he preferred to hold to his original ideas.

Now he felt a surge of annoyance as he looked at Rutter's mashed features. In only a few days, he had planned to give the signal to start the big freight wagons rolling down out of the Diablos with their cargoes of destruction. But Rutter's clumsiness in handling Killian and in handling the drifter—Marne, he remembered someone calling him—these were threatening Doncaster's plan.

He said abruptly, "If it hadn't been for Carnap's recognizing that army man, he'd have tricked you good!"

Then, as if he had vented enough of his temper for one time, he said in a more even tone, "I want Carnap to get a look at the drifter. Route him out and send him back to the posada."

"And if he is army?"

"I want him brought here. I don't want him killed—not yet," Doncaster said. He grunted at Rutter's obvious puzzlement. "I want him brought here, no matter who or what he is. I want to know why he's in this valley. If he's army, I want to know how the word got out that brought him here. A dead man can't tell us how much the enemy knows. A live one can."

Rutter heaved himself painfully to his feet. "I'll send Pike along with Carnap. Fitz is a better man, but he's got a crew out hunting for Killian."

"And they'd better find him soon," Doncaster said with soft savagery.

"They will," Rutter said quickly. "He's got to come out again for food. And Fitz claims he was winged yesterday.

That means he might be running for Arroyo Verde to get patched up. With every way out of these crazy mountains blocked off, he hasn't got a chance."

"If that's so, what happened to the man who helped Killian?"

"He'll turn up," Rutter said confidently. "Unless," he added with a grin, "he ran his horse over a canyon in the dark. Then we might not find him for quite a spell."

"Guessing isn't enough!" Doncaster snapped. "I want to know." He curbed himself again with an obvious effort. "We're too close to moving out. We can't afford any more mistakes. Not one. Once we get the wagons rolling, once we get the men hitting and the Indians raiding, then be damned to the army. Nothing will stop us."

His voice dropped to a whisper. "When I get through with these territories, the government will wish they'd shot me eight years back. Before we're done, there won't be a white settler from the divide to the Colorado River—except the ones I let come in!"

"And gold in our pockets," Rutter said. "Don't forget the gold."

"Don't *you* forget it," Doncaster said. His voice was level again. "One mistake can cause you and the men to lose everything. Now get out of here and start Carnap on his way to town. And tomorrow I want to have that drifter here to talk to, and I want that army man to look at—dead!"

Marne pressed tightly to the adobe wall of the posada and listened to the rapid Spanish coming from the room above him. From the sound of Marita's voice, she was obviously shocked by her grandfather's declaration that he would kill Marne if the CR ordered him to.

She said quickly, "What good is all of this, *abuelo?* Are we to spend the rest of our lives afraid of these men? Living like animals afraid to come out of our holes?"

"There are more lives than ours to consider," the old man said.

"But if there was a chance for them, too—what then?" she

demanded. She rushed on. "There are two men here, one from the army, the other the one you saw tonight. Both are fighting men. Let them help us. This is our chance to take back our own so that we can stand up and face these—these animals."

The sheriff sounded angry. "The other man is still in the Diablos? You hid him against my orders? And now you say he is of the army!"

"I wasn't going to let him die," Marita flared.

"Nor I," Tonio said quietly. "She is right, *abuelo*. It is time we fought these carrion. And the Lieutenant Killian and the one who calls himself Marne—if they help . . ."

"You can trust this man Marne? You can know he is not one of them?"

"I am sure he is not," Marita said.

"I—almost," Tonio said. "Sometimes I think he is, but then I see the face of Rutter smashed and bleeding. I do not think it was pretense to fool us." He paused and added, "Besides, if we are wrong, if he is one of them, I will be with him all the time. I can kill him quickly enough."

"You're talking like children," the old man said. "Your Lieutenant Killian is hiding somewhere. This man Marne is running. And you, Tonio, will have to run also. Do you think Rutter will forgive what you did tonight in the cantina?"

"I will take Marne to Killian," Tonio said in sudden decision. "If he is hurt, we will wait until he is healed. We will plan a way to help our people, and then we will get word to you."

"I cannot risk it," the old man said. "If Rutter or that man Doncaster even suspects . . ." He broke off and began again. "You know what they will do."

Marita spoke to him, but so softly that Marne could not catch the words. Then Marne heard the tired voice say, "You are right, *chiquita*. We have no choice if we are to live again. I will do as you say."

His voice saddened. "To think that two years ago when this man Doncaster came into these mountains we showed him courtesy. We fed him and helped him on his way."

"Such things happen," Tonio said fatalistically. His footsteps approached the window. He leaned out. "Go to the ground. I will meet you there. We will ride away together."

Marne lifted a hand to indicate he had understood. He heard the old man's brief, explosive irritation at the realization that Marne had been close by all the time. Then it faded as the sound of horses coming fast toward the posada filled the air.

"The men from the CR," the sheriff said. "I told them I would bring Marne to them. They have grown impatient. Hurry, Tonio. I will tell them something while you ride away."

Before the riders reached the front of the posada, Marne was on the ground and hurrying toward the rear of a large yard, his warbag bouncing on his shoulder. He stopped and stood pressed into shadow, waiting for Tonio Potrero.

The boy came quickly, his arms loaded with his gear. He stepped up beside Marne and whispered, "It is the one called Carnap. The one who escaped from prison. And a man named Pike. He already killed one of our people. We must hurry."

Marne realized that Tonio had forgotten that he was not supposed to understand Spanish, and the boy assumed he knew the plans. Marne did not waste the time to point this out now. Besides, he was not sure there was any point in further pretense. He said only, "Our horses?"

"Marita will bring them while the *abuelo* holds off the men," Tonio replied. He faded quietly through a gate, leaving Marne to follow.

They slipped down an alley, thick with mountain darkness. A short run across an open space and then they were protected by a high adobe wall. When they finally stopped, it took Marne a moment to orient himself. He realized they were behind the church.

"Where do you figure on going?" Marne whispered.

"Tonight to a cave nearby. Tomorrow, we will ride to Tim Killian. After that—*quién sabe?*"

Who did know, Marne wondered. If they got through

60

country swarming with CR men, and if they found Tim Killian alive—then it would be time to make further plans.

Suddenly the quietness of the night was torn by a deep-voiced shout. "You there! Where are you going with them horses?"

Tonio swore in Spanish. "They have seen Marita bringing us the horses!" he whispered in anguish.

Before Marne could answer, a gun crashed and a horse neighed in fright. Marne jerked his gun free and ran around the corner of the church and into the open.

X

As MARNE SWUNG around the corner of the church, a dark figure crouched over a small chestnut pony swept within feet of him. The rider was Marita, he saw, and she had two saddled horses strung out behind her, like pack animals. From the edge of his eye, he saw her whip out of sight. He lifted his head as the close hammering of heavy hoofs battered at his ears.

Two riders were driving their horses across the middle of the plaza. Dim starlight flickered off gun metal and then flame spurted as one of the men fired in the direction Marita had taken. The bullet whined inches from Marne as he moved swiftly into shadow. Deliberately, he lifted his .44 and sent two shots screaming inches above the riders' hats. From the corner of the church, Tonio's gun opened up.

Now the men reined their horses in sharply, sending hoofs clawing the air. The horses settled down and the lead rider thrust himself forward, peering into the shadows, his gun held ready. Marne carefully pitched his voice higher than normal.

"Back off," he called. "Get out of town or the next shots won't be over your heads!"

"Who the devil are you?" the man cried. Although Marne

could not see his features clearly, he recognized the nasal tones of the man he had picked up in the desert the night Doncaster escaped. This was Carnap.

"The man you're looking for," Marne said mockingly. "Go tell your boss that if he wants me, he'll have to come and get me himself."

Tonio had moved close to Marne. "You are crazy," he whispered. "You are angering them!"

"My intention," Marne said softly. "I can't wait around all night. They'll either fight or ride—and I'm going to make them decide which it'll be."

"This is the CR," Carnap shouted. "Now step out here, and bring that kid with you. We're taking a ride, mister. The boss wants to talk to you. So make up your mind to it."

"If that's what he wants, tell him to send a man to get the job done," Marne taunted deliberately. "Now ride out before you have to be carried home!"

Carnap started his horse slowly forward. Tonio put a hand on Marne's arm. "You dare not shoot, *señor*," he said pleadingly. "Not to hit them. Please, for our sake. . . ."

From the corner of the building, Marita's voice came in a commanding whisper. "The horses are waiting. You can ride away."

Marne said angrily, "I can make them ride too. What's wrong with fighting back?"

"Nothing," she snapped. "But this is not the time. The *abuelo* became frightened at what he was doing. He refuses to help us more. In a few moments, he may even come and be on their side. Please, do not fight here. Not now."

Marne looked at Carnap coming slowly, steadily toward him. He hated to turn tail and run. Yet, until he knew why the sheriff was acting this way, why Marita and Tonio were so concerned—until then, he could not be sure he was doing right by taking matters into his own hands.

He motioned Tonio to slide back around the corner. Then, reluctantly, he followed, hugging the shadow and moving quietly so as not to alert Carnap to what was happening.

Marita motioned to Marne's horse and to a leggy sorrel that

obviously belonged to Tonio. Marne climbed into the saddle. "How do we get out of here?" He looked around. There was little ground behind the church. A few short feet away, the hill started. It rose abruptly, too steep to climb. On the far side of the adobe building, the slope came down against the wall.

"There is a tunnel," Marita said. "Our ancestors used it when banditos attacked in an effort to take away the silver. This was many years ago, but the tunnel remains."

Marne rode to the corner of the church and carefully peered around. Carnap was less than fifty feet away now. He nodded to Marita. "Lead the way."

Tonio said, "We must tie the horses together as before. Otherwise, you could get lost, *señor*. It will be very dark."

Marne let the dun be tied to Marita's saddle. Tonio came behind him. Then Marita led the way. She rode directly toward the far corner of the building, where the thickly bushed hillside came squeezing down against the adobe walls. They were almost into the break in the bushes before Marne saw it and the dark opening behind it. Then they were in a wide, musty-smelling tunnel, and there was no more light.

Marne felt the darkness squeeze in on him and his nerves tingled. He did not like being shut up, away from the open sweep of sky and land. And this was worse than the narrowest of deep canyons. This was blindness. The plop of horses' hoofs against damp earth and the steady sound of water dripping echoed against his ear drums. The air grew chill and dank, and the musty, unused smell became stronger.

When Marne said, "Where does this thing come out?" his voice echoed strangely in his ears.

"Above the posada," Tonio replied from behind him. "The main shaft of the mines once began there. This is a side shaft."

Hoofs splashed through water now. Marne wondered how deep it was. A chill drop slid down from above and found its way under his collar and along his back. He twitched as if a knifeblade had been laid across his skin.

"I'd rather fight a dozen CR men than do this again," he said.

"It is not much longer," Marita assured him.

Marne wanted to talk to keep his mind from the thick, blanketing blackness. "How do you keep from getting lost?"

"All the other side tunnels have been blocked off," Tonio answered. "We can only go the one way. And when I was a boy, I ran a rope from one end of this tunnel to the other. It is as high as a man on a horse. Marita uses it to guide herself."

Marne reached out with his right hand and felt nothing. He thrust out his left. His fingers touched damp stone. He felt the roughness of rope slide across his knuckles. He drew his hand back.

"Did they recognize you, Marita?"

"No. I was too far away. They did not see me until I was halfway across the plaza from the livery barn. They could see that I led two horses. That is why they knew I was helping you to escape."

"But if they guess it was you—what then?"

"There would be trouble," she admitted. "That is why we must hurry. We must find Tim—the Señor Killian. And then we must make a plan to . . ."

"Quiet," Tonio said suddenly. "There is light ahead. Stop and I will go forward and see if it is clear."

The chestnut and the dun both stopped. Marne felt Tonio untie his sorrel. In a moment Tonio had squeezed past the other horses. One moment Marne saw the faint slit of dimness that meant the end of the tunnel; the next, it was blotted out by Tonio and his horse.

The boy's voice came back: *"Seguro."*

Marita started up the chestnut, drawing the dun after her. Marne watched eagerly as the dimness returned and then grew. Finally he broke out of the musty darkness into the sharp, cool air of the mountain night. The moon was well behind a hill but its radiance reflected across the sky looked like the sun. The stars he could see were bright candles, warm and cheering. He sucked in a deep breath of relief.

"Now what?"

"I will return to the posada," Marita said. "You must find Tim quickly. When he is well, it will be time to act."

She nodded as she untied the chestnut from the dun. Reining around, she galloped toward the mouth of the small canyon they were in and disappeared. Tonio pointed upslope. "There is a cave. We will sleep there."

"Sleep? I thought we were going after Killian."

"*Sí, mañana.* It is very dangerous to go to him in the dark. We will start at daybreak. And the horses will be fresh, also."

Silently, Marne followed him along the twisting canyon bottom, glad for the moonlight that angled down here and allowed them to see their way over the treacherous footing. They passed the wide mouth of a sandy-bottomed arroyo.

Tonio gestured toward it. "That leads to the rear of the posada." A short way on, he turned north, into a narrow, high-cliffed cul de sac. At the end was a shallow cave, little more than a deep overhang. A tiny spring trickled at one side, forming a pool. The water spilled onto the floor of the little gully and brought up lush, almost rank grass.

"There is food for the horses," Tonio said proudly. "Sand to lay our blankets on. Water to wash down our meals."

Marne dropped to the ground and began to strip the saddle from the dun. "We've got everything we want," he said slowly. He paused and added, "Except for one thing."

Tonio glanced at him. "One thing, Señor Marne?"

"Mutual trust," Marne said.

XI

THE DAY APPEARED cloudless, the air winey. Marne felt rested, despite the few short hours of sleep, and he ate as much as he felt could be spared from the rations packed in their saddlebags. By the time they were ready to ride, the sun had begun to angle into this maze of canyons, and Marne showed his impatience to be on the trail.

65

"How do we go?" he asked, lifting himself into the saddle. "I don't know this piece of country, but my guess is that canyon we turned from last night will lead us to the trail going out north."

Tonio nodded. "Where the canyon trail meets the road, another trail starts on the far side. It too goes deep into the hills and very close to the CR ranch."

"I know that trail!" Marne exclaimed. "It'll be the one that goes into those barrancas over to the west." He grinned suddenly. "That's where Tim must be. There are some hide holes there that would take a man with a map a week to find."

Tonio studied him with suspicion again plain on his face. "You seem to know much about these mountains."

"I was here two years ago," Marne said. He debated whether to explain himself, and he decided to the devil with it. If Tonio could not take him at face value, he wasn't going to force himself on the boy.

Tonio led the way into the narrow canyon and westward along its twisting course. He turned suddenly and stared at Marne. "Ay!" he said. "The *abuelo* was right when he told me he thought you might be the one who was here two years ago—looking for Doncaster."

Marne grimaced. "He still has sharp eyes. I had a beard then."

A look close to triumph shone in Tonio's eyes. "At that time, you said you were looking for a friend. Now you say that Doncaster is not a friend. How are we to believe?"

Marne said flatly, "I was in the army. Doncaster was an escaped prisoner—as Carnap is today. What would the sheriff have done if I had told him that the army wanted to catch Doncaster to hang him?"

Tonio's expression told Marne that he had guessed right as to the temperament of these people. To them, the army represented an authority they did not understand and one they were not sure they could trust. Under Spanish and later Mexican rule, the army had meant only one thing—an arrogant disregard for personal rights. The army collected ex-

66

cessive taxes. The army looted. The army helped itself to the village girls, to the people's food and wine. It commandeered the best houses.

This, Marne knew, would be the way the sheriff thought. He was old enough to remember the early days. But it would not be the way Tonio and Marita thought. It did not explain their fear of army men.

Marne said now, suddenly, "I don't know why you're afraid of the U.S. cavalry coming here. But Tim Killian told me you and Marita were so afraid of the army that you would have turned him in if you'd known at first he was a Lieutenant. If I was one of Rutter's men, I would know." He looked straight at Tonio and said in quick, liquid Spanish, "*Verdad?*"

The strength of the argument was not lost on Tonio. He said, "It could be true, *sí*." And then the realization that Marne had spoken to him in Spanish struck his consciousness. The suspicion that had thickened his tone wavered. "If the army should come here to help us, what we have worked to save would be lost." He was speaking Spanish now and Marne nodded at intervals to let it be known that he understood.

"That is why none of my people have left the Diablos," Tonio went on. "We, too, know the way across the big rock. But why should we leave? We can do nothing away from here."

"And you do nothing here," Marne said harshly. "I always thought the sheriff a brave man. But before Rutter's cowhands, he is nothing. *Nada!*"

Tonio said softly, "You too would be so with men such as they, Señor Marne—if your *hija* and your *mujer* and your grandchildren were held prisoner. If they would be killed when you did not do as you were told."

Marne stared at him. "Rutter has the sheriff's wife as a hostage?"

"*Sí*. My grandmother, my aunt, my two young cousins. They work for him. They cook and clean. They bring water. They sweep the stables. Now and then one of us has visited them. Then we see how tired they are from such work, and how frightened. Men like Rutter and Doncaster would do as they promised—and kill them. Human life means nothing."

Now Marne could understand the sheriff's terrible problem. And he admired the man for having, even on only a few occasions, flared up and tried to fight back. And he admired Tonio and Marita as well. He knew how strong was the sense of family among these people.

Marne said, "Now I know why Tim Killian wouldn't leave the Diablos. He knew the true story, didn't he?"

Again suspicion flared in Tonio's eyes. "He did not tell you—a friend?"

"He told me he didn't know. I suspect he was lying to keep a promise to you."

Tonio smiled briefly. "He promised us he would not leave the mountains until he had helped us fight the CR. And he promised to tell no one of the trouble—our trouble."

"He kept that promise," Marne said dryly. He knew that for all of Tonio's frankness at the moment, his own fate was hanging by the thinnest of spider's silk. Tonio had only three choices—he could take Marne at face value and accept his story, or he could believe what he had believed earlier, that Marne was a spy for Rutter, or he could think that Marne was still in the army. In the first case, Tonio would probably go on helping Marne find Killian. In the second, his only sensible move would be to get rid of Marne in such a way that the CR couldn't blame him. And if he chose to believe the third, he might also try to get rid of Marne, if only to make sure that he didn't get out of the mountains and bring the army back.

He wished he could know now what was going on in Tonio's mind. But the youthful, olive-toned features were expressionless. Tonio seemed at the moment to be concentrating on following the tortuous bottom of the canyon.

He said suddenly, "Soon we will reach the wagon road. After we cross it, the traveling will be easier. But follow me closely. It is easy to get lost."

"And you think I might try to do just that?"

Tonio's expression remained noncommittal. Marne went

on, "You play a good game of poker, but I think I can read your mind. You're wondering two things about me—why I didn't admit before that I speak Spanish, and whether or not I might try to get out of the Diablos and go get the army's help."

"I think these things, *sí,*" Tonio admitted.

"I learn a lot when people don't think I understand their language," Marne said. "But now the time has come when you must trust me. I need your help—for Tim Killian. So I let you know this about me." His Spanish was fluent and strong with an accent similar to Tonio's. It obviously pleased the boy.

Marne went on. "I also will tell you that I am still in the army."

"Ah! Then this Colonel sent you to find Tim Killian!"

"No," Marne said. "I am officially on leave. I came here for myself, with no legal rights. I came to get Doncaster before he causes too much trouble."

"I would like to believe that," Tonio said softly. "But if it is true, then you will ride away and report the trouble here and . . ."

"No," Marne said. "I came to find Doncaster. I won't leave without him. And once he's my prisoner, then you will no longer have the trouble. I promise I will stay and fight."

Tonio's teeth flashed in a quick grin of appreciation. "*Gracias, amigo.*"

Marne grinned back. Then his eye caught movement ahead and his whole attention turned to what lay before them. The trail had become smoother suddenly as the walls of the canyon widened. Marne could see over Tonio's shoulder at a piece of the dusty wagonroad running north from the town of Arroyo Verde down to the desert and finally on to El Paso, a good many miles to the east. On the far side of the tiny strip of road visible to Marne was a stand of low bushes backed by fat piñon and juniper trees. It was movement of the bushes that caught Marne's attention.

He whispered hoarsely, "Tonio, turn back!"

The command in his voice brought Tonio reining his horse

around just before it would have stepped onto the road. Marne backed the dun until both of them were back around the first bend.

"Someone is in those bushes straight across," Marne said.

Now hoofbeats hammered on the wagonroad as a rider came from the north. Marne drew his carbine from the saddle boot. But the sounds faded without any CR man appearing in the canyon.

Then the clatter of a metal shoe on rock swiveled both Marne and Tonio's heads upward. Tonio swore softly. "They are trying to get in position to shoot down on us!"

A grin flickered across Marne's flat mouth. "They're not careful enough," he said. "A good Indian would have their scalps in jig time." He motioned for Tonio to move closer.

"Listen," Marne whispered. "The joker up there can't get a good angle on us without exposing himself. But he can make it hot enough to force us to ride in one direction or the other. My guess is he'll try to send us out on the road where his friends can pick us off easily."

Tonio had his handgun out. Both he and Marne were silent as they listened to the movement above them. A small rock rattled down the cliff face as the man up on the rim worked to get a position where he could fire down at them.

"It is safest to ride back the way we have come," Tonio said softly.

"And then?" Marne demanded. "How is that going to get us to Tim Killian?" He saw Tonio's grimace of comprehension and went on, "Turn your horse again toward the road. Keep an eye on the ridge up there. I'll start riding. That'll make the joker above try to move out to get a shot at me. Then you'll have an angle on him."

Tonio frowned. "I do not understand."

Marne said quickly, almost impatiently, "If you can put the one on the ridge out of commission, the odds will be better for us. I'll keep on riding—right out into the road. I'll start spraying lead as soon as I leave the canyon. You come right behind me. With luck we can surprise whoever's waiting for us and get into the hills on the other side."

ricocheting bullet whined up from the surface of the road and scoured a hot finger across the dun's flank. The bony horse jerked, nearly unseating Marne, and then raced straight for the waiting gunman to the north.

Marne was close enough to see the stubby carbine barrel poking at him through the bushes. He swung the dun with a violent jerk of the reins, sending it straight north along the road. This brought him broadside to the man in the bushes, and now he brought his .44 around and sent a spray of lead screaming through the leaves and branches of the undergrowth.

Marne heard the rider crash backwards, and then he was racing on past. He was almost out of range before the man in the bushes managed to get into position on the road and drive a shot after him. The half spent bullet buzzed by Marne's hat. He twisted in the saddle to see one of the CR men on horseback and the other still on foot.

He could hear the man on horseback shouting at the one who had come out of the bushes but he was too far away to catch more than a rumble of sound. Frowning, Marne slowed the dun's breakneck pace. Neither of the CR men seemed interested in chasing him. After disappearing for a moment, the man who had been on foot appeared again; but now he was mounted and, with his partner, he swung his horse after Marne. Yet neither man hurried his mount.

They acted, Marne thought, as if they were out for a Sunday ride. Or as if they could corral him any time they chose to. He looked at the trail winding northward ahead of him. A low rise lay not far beyond. And after that, he recalled, the land made a long, steady but gentle slope downward to the edge of the mountain benchland. Then it dropped sharply and suddenly down to the desert of this part of New Mexico Territory.

He looked about him, and then he understood why the men behind him were not hurrying. Fifteen to twenty foot high cliffs rose on both sides of the road. And they ran without a break as far to the north as he could see. He shut off his eyes, squeezing memory into view behind his eyelids.

Cliffs as far as the other side of the low pass. And then?
Then, he remembered, the cliff lifted on the left, while on the
right the road's edge dropped suddenly, violently, into the
depths of a canyon.

He couldn't go back, Marne thought grimly. He had no
way of leaving the trail, either to the east or the west. He
could only go ahead, into the desert.

He swore suddenly as the full realization of what was
happening here struck him. What had Tim Killian said?—
that the CR had a crew of guards posted at the point where
this north road started its drop down to the desert!

He was boxed in—with CR men waiting in front and coming up from behind, slowly and steadily, their guns catching
bright sunlight as the barrels bobbed up and down, lifted
and dropped where they rested on the saddlebows.

XII

TONIO CROUCHED in the mouth of the canyon, his gun ready
to help Marne. But at first Marne and the dun were in the
way, blocking out any shot he might have at the targets
across the road, and then Marne was spurring the dun forward, firing as he went—and for a moment there was no one
for Tonio to shoot at.

Then suddenly a man came riding from the screen of trees.
Another man appeared a bit to the north, lifted his carbine,
and sent a shot winging toward Marne. Tonio lifted his gun,
steadying it for a shot at the man on foot, the one closer to
Marne.

His aim wavered and then his gun barrel sagged as the
man on horseback cried, "Don't hit him, you fool! You know
the boss's orders."

He laughed sharply as the other man lowered his gun.
"Go get your horse," he ordered, "and we'll mosey up the
trail a-ways. I figure we ought to be meeting on the other

side of that hump, about where the boys'll be waiting on the edge of the bench."

Tonio turned away, fighting a burst of bitter anger. He had brought himself so close to believing in this man Marne! He had let himself be talked out of his suspicions. And all the time he had been right. That man's words made it plain enough. Marne was one of them! Tonio couldn't understand what Marne's purpose in his actions to date had been, but at the moment it didn't matter. He had almost fooled Tonio into taking him to Tim Killian, into revealing the hiding place of the one outside friend the people of Arroyo Verde had.

And, Tonio thought suddenly, Marne still had Marita believing in him. What if after the meeting with his friends he should swing back to the posada and get her to help him find Tim Killian. She trusted Marne now, Tonio knew. Marne could explain his—Tonio's—absence by some plausible story and then he and the CR would have Marita helping them!

He must warn Marita as quickly as possible. And then . . . ?

Then he had to get to Tim Killian and help him find another place to hide. Marne, Tonio recalled, had guessed the army man's hiding place and he, like a fool, had as good as admitted that Marne was right!

He saw his horse lying a short distance away. It was obviously dead and without a further look at it, Tonio began to run. A half dozen strides up the canyon and suddenly he found himself sprawled on his face on the rough ground. Stupidly, he came to his feet. His left leg felt strange, threatening to collapse under him, and he stared down at it.

For the first time, he realized he was wounded. The bullet that had killed his horse had first smashed across his leg, ripping his jeans and leaving a savage burn in the flesh of his thigh. And now he could feel the pain beginning.

Cursing harshly in Spanish, Tonio turned and limped slowly back to the dead horse. He worked his saddlebags free and found in one the bandages and grease dressing he sought. He had taken it for Tim Killian's wound, but now he used it for himself.

With a heavy bandage around his thigh, he found he could

move more easily. But his progress was slow, and he realized that at this pace it would be too late by the time he reached the posada. Marne on horseback could have reached her, taken her away, and be well on the trail to where Tim Killian was hiding.

Teeth clenched, Tonio tried to step his pace up to a jog. But the pounding from the rough ground soon had him walking again. His only chance, he realized, was to get a horse. He looked up at the ridge, cursing the man who had shot his mount dead.

The cursing stopped and he grinned suddenly. What about that one's horse? He had not walked up to that ridge. And from the way he had fallen back the second time, he would not need any way of getting to where he was going. Ghosts did not need horses, at least not to ride to hell.

Up ahead, a narrow, steep trail twisted up the cliff face to the ridge. Tonio surveyed it from the bottom, his expression dubious. It was one thing to scramble up it, as he had more than once, but it would be another to make the climb with a bullet-burned leg.

But he had no choice. Sucking in his breath, he set himself to the climb. The carbine and the saddlebags he had slung over his shoulder encumbered him, but he clung grimly to them. He wanted the saddlebags for the food and medicine they contained. He wanted the gun because there was just a chance that he might meet Marne trying to return to the posada.

A year ago, he thought, he had made this climb in less than ten minutes. Now it was a half hour and he had to belly down at the top to wait for the strength to come back to him. Finally he was able to get to his feet, and he looked across the grassy, tree-dotted flat. He saw a flicker of movement and walked toward it. A gray horse appeared from behind a small piñon and moved awkwardly toward him. It was saddled and hobbled.

In five minutes he was on the animal's back. He rode toward the edge of the canyon, stopping when he found the lean, slack-jawed man who had wounded him and killed his horse. The man was dead. Tonio crossed himself and rode on toward a high point to the west.

From a knoll top he could look out over the wagonroad. It was visible as far as the low pass to the north and almost to Arroyo Verde to the south. Tonio felt a tug of disappointment. He had hoped to see Marne riding within carbine range.

He reined the gray about and stepped up its pace until the throbbing of his leg told him it could handle no more. He held the horse just below this speed, working it eastward along the flat, down a steep, short pitch into a canyon, and through a twisting maze of eroded land until finally he was back on the trail that led to the rear of the posada.

He did not expect any more CR men to be near town at this time of day, but he took no chances, leaving the gray well hidden and limping the last few hundred yards to the building. He found Marita directing the preparation of the noonday meal.

She stared at him in surprise. "Tonio, what are you doing here? Where is the Señor Marne?"

"That one!" Tonio spat. "He is with his friends by this time. And soon he will lead them to where Tim Killian waits. If he does not take the time to come here first—for your help."

"What are you talking about?" she demanded.

"I am saying that your Señor Marne is what I thought he was—a spy sent by Rutter and Doncaster to trap us into helping them find Tim Killian."

And while she continued to stare at him, he poured out his story—what he had seen and heard, what he had guessed, and what he feared Marne would do.

"I cannot believe you," Marita said flatly. "He was not that kind of man. He does not seem the same as those men from the CR."

"A woman's foolishness," Tonio said with heavy scorn. He stepped toward a table to pick up a freshly cooked tortilla. He gasped as pain tore through his leg. His muscles gave way and he half fell, keeping himself erect only by grabbing the table edge.

Marita was beside him quickly, solicitously. "Tonio?"

"It is nothing," he said. "Only a bullet burn. I will dress it again before I go."

Brushing aside his protestations, she led him into another room. "Before you go where?" she demanded.

"I cannot stay here," Tonio reminded her. "Also, I must find Tim Killian and warn him."

While he talked, Marita deftly slit his trouser leg and cut away the bandage. She looked at the bullet burn, swollen and angry red around the edges now.

"You will go nowhere until that is better," she said flatly. "We will hide you here where Elena and Pablo can take care of you."

"Sí, and while I am hiding like a rabbit, this man Marne is killing our friend!"

"I will ride to him," Marita said quickly. "I know the Diablos as well as you." She walked away, leaving his protests hanging in the air.

After arranging for Elena and Pablo to take care of Tonio, Marita hurriedly dressed in her riding clothes and prepared a pack of the necessities she judged she would need. She felt little immediate concern for Tonio. He was in good hands—since she could remember, Elena and Pablo had been quietly running the posada behind the scenes, keeping the servants working, doctoring animals and people, and watching out for the innumerable small, curious children that always seemed to be about.

Marita saddled her leggy sorrel. She paused, one foot lifted to the stirrup. Slowly she let her foot back down. Where, she wondered, did she go from here? What should she do first? She found it hard to believe that Tonio was right about Marne—she could not think of him as the kind of man who would deliberately trick people into betraying a friend. There was a quality about him that reminded her of Tim Killian; and when she thought of him, a smile lifted the corners of her mouth and warmed the glow of her dark eyes.

She shook her head, angry with herself. Mooning like a schoolgirl when there was work to be done—important work. She must do two things, she decided. She must find out the truth about Marne and she must get to Tim as quickly as possible. If Tonio was right, then she would have to hurry even more to Tim, as Marne now knew the part of the mountains where he was hiding. But if Tonio was wrong, if Marne was not one of the CR men, then she would try to get him to help her. It would be better that way, especially if they found Tim badly wounded.

Mounting the sorrel, Marita started away from the town by following the same route Tonio and Marne had taken last night. She rode this stretch of country automatically, without concerning herself about direction. She had ridden it many times before, and both she and the sorrel knew it without having to think where they were going.

Marita frowned as her mind turned to Tonio's accusation. There were two things that made her cousin's fears absurd, she thought. If Marne was a CR man and if he had gone to all that trouble to gain their confidence so that he could find Tim Killian, why would he bother to come back to the posada for her? No, Tonio was imagining again. He was building huge castles from small houses, as he had always done since his childhood.

She smiled with soft affection at the memory of Tonio's weaknesses, then her frown returned as the problem came harshly back. The second thing that made her question Tonio's judgement was the way Marne had acted since coming to Arroyo Verde. She could not believe he would have fought so with Rutter if they had been pretending. Nor could she believe that Rutter would have let himself be humiliated so—not even if Doncaster ordered him to.

Marne, she said to herself, had a right to be judged further.

Reasoning that if Marne and the CR men had ridden north along the wagonroad, they would have to come back along it a good distance when they went to the CR, she rode up onto the ridge where Tonio had taken the horse.

THE HOLDOUT IN THE DIABLOS

Leaving the sorrel, Marita climbed on foot to the highest point on the ridge—a stubby rock thrusting up from a low hill. From here she could see as far as the low pass to the north, and in that direction the road was empty. Her eyes moved westward, following the trails that branched from the wagonroad to lead to the CR and to the hills beyond it.

And now she saw them—three miniature figures riding single file. They were too far away for her to recognize faces, but only one of the horses was a solid color, and that was dun. The horse in the middle, she saw. That would be Marne. He must be their prisoner, then. Otherwise he would be in the lead, showing the way to Tim Killian's hiding place. She hurried back to the sorrel. She had one chance—to help Marne before his captors reached the safety of the CR!

XIII

MARITA DARED NOT follow Marne and the CR men directly, and once across the wagonroad, she put her horse onto a steep side trail that would bring her onto their trail some quarter mile from the CR itself. She hesitated before taking the shortcut; it was a dangerous trail, now hanging on the edge of a deep canyon, now twisting its way through narrow bottoms where one of the sudden mountain thunderstorms could send a slash of water down with killing force. But she saw no other hope of getting near enough to Marne in time.

It was with a sense of relief that she rode the sorrel out of the last narrow gully and reined it in behind a high shoulder of rock edging the trail leading to the CR. She sat quietly now, listening to the sorrel's breathing and trying to hear the clop of hoofs that would warn her of the men's coming.

She gasped as she realized suddenly that she had no plan at all in mind. What would she do when they came? What could she do if Marne turned out as Tonio claimed—to be one of them? She drew her carbine from the saddle boot and laid the barrel over her leg. She checked the load and then let her hands rest quietly on the stock.

Her mind moved from possibility to possibility, rejecting each one. She realized finally that she had only one real solution to her problem. She had to find out which side Marne really held his allegiance to. She was not a violent person and the risk that answering the question involved frightened her a little. But she had come too far along this trail to turn back now. She would do what must be done.

Now that her decision was made, she listened impatiently for the sound of the men's coming. She heard the hoofbeats at last. They echoed from the left and less than fifty yards away, she judged. She thumbed back the safety on her carbine. With whispered words she calmed the sorrel as she moved it closer to the corner of the rock. The clatter of hoofs on the rocky surface of the trail grew louder. Now she could hear the jangle of harness. Then a voice rose, startling her.

"I about got it figured out. Just give me a little more time. I got an ear for voices and an eye for faces."

The words had no meaning to Marita, but she recognized the tone. The speaker was Carnap, the one who had escaped from Fort Douglas, the one Tim Killian had come here to find. He was a man she had disliked on sight, not only for his physical ugliness but because of the arrogant way he looked at her and her people. If she had to shoot at anyone, she hoped her target would be Carnap.

There was no answer to his words. In a moment the first horse passed across Marita's view of the trail. The long, bony face, the drooping mustache over the loose mouth, and the pulled down left eyelid were unmistakable. This was Carnap in the lead. Close behind him came Marne on his dun. She studied him intently, noticing the easy, almost relaxed way he sat the saddle, noticing the fact that his handgun was still in its holster and his carbine in its boot. It was not until his body almost hid her view that she realized part of his relaxed appearance was because he rode with his hands over the saddle horn, the reins held lightly in his fingers. And, she realized with a sudden jolt of excitement, he guided the horse that way because his wrists were lashed to the horn!

She had her answer and she could change her plan. But there was no time. The third man, a chunky, bearded cowhand she knew as Fitz, was already coming into sight. And he rode with his .44 in one hand, the barrel resting on his saddlebow, his finger very near the trigger.

Sucking in a deep breath, Marita lifted her carbine. She deepened her voice as much as she could manage and let out a wild, Indian-like shout. At the same time, she fired the carbine rapidly twice. The first bullet she sent deliberately scouring the rump of Fitz's horse; the second she tried to put above Carnap's head, but her aim was low and she drilled a hole high in the crown of his hat.

Fitz' horse leaped as the bullet burned its hide. It sunfished once, sending the chunky CR man clawing for air, whaling at the sky with his gun, and finally landing belly down on the rough trail.

Carnap shouted, "Indians, by God!" in a surprised voice, and put spurs to his horse. It clattered uptrail, hoofs sending sparks from the rocky ground.

He would recover in a moment, Marita knew. And so would Fitz. Neither man was a coward nor a fool. The absurdity of an Indian attack would dawn on them both. But by then, she hoped to be well away.

She called now in Spanish, "Sígame, amigo. Pronto! Prontísimo, sígame."

The shout and the sound of the carbine had confused Marne at first. Then he saw the hole appear in Carnap's hat and he heard Fitz' curse as he was flung off his horse. Thinking the attacker was either Tonio or Killian, he was already working the reins awkwardly in his fingers in an effort to turn when an obviously feminine voice told him to follow and to do it now.

He didn't let his surprise at seeing Marita at the edge of the rock slow him down. Using both his fingers on the reins and his knees, Marne headed the dun in her direction. As the horse went past, Marita grabbed the reins. "I will lead!" she said. She put her heels to her horse's flanks.

Marne glanced back in time to see Fitz rise and stare after them. "He saw us take this trail," he called.

"It does not matter," Marita replied. "Soon we will be where they would not think to go."

"If you'll stop and cut my hands loose, we can get there faster," Marne said.

"Sí." Marita reined in, turned and rode alongside Marne. She drew a small hunting knife she carried at her belt and slashed the thongs binding his wrists. She turned away, saying cryptically, "Now I will know for sure."

Before Marne could ask her what she meant, she had spurred the sorrel well ahead. He set the dun the task of following over the narrow, twisting, unfamiliar terrain. Soon he saw her pause where two of the gullies came together. She glanced back, lifted a hand to him, and reined to her left. When Marne reached the spot, he found himself looking at what seemed to be solid rock, covered with low bushes at the base and reaching high toward the sharp blue of the sky.

He bent, studying the ground. But it was too covered with flinty rock to show any sign. He began to move slowly along the rock face, and just as he saw the slit-like opening that seemed to be no more than shadow from the rough surface, he heard her call him. By making a sharp turn, he managed to squeeze the dun and his own legs through the narrow opening. He found himself in a fairly wide, sand-bottomed arroyo. Marita was waiting.

"There is a small spring ahead," she said. "We will rest the horses there." Turning, she sent the sorrel on ahead.

The spring was less than two hundred yards ahead, a bare trickle of water that worked out of rock and into a small pool. Dismounting, Marita and Marne drank, then led the horses forward.

"Thanks for the help," Marne said. He rubbed the thong marks on his wrists as he looked down at her. "But exactly what are you doing here? Where's Tonio?"

"I am here because Tonio has been wounded," she said. "Not badly, but enough to keep him away. Besides," she added in a flat voice, "he would not have helped you. He thinks you are a spy, that you are one of the CR."

"Still!" Marne swallowed a desire to swear at the boy. "Didn't he see . . ."

She interrupted. "He saw and he heard. That is why he suspects." Quickly, she told him what Tonio had told her.

As he listened, Marne noticed the way she watched him. She herself was not yet sure, he realized. And now he understood the meaning of her cryptic remark of a short time ago. He admired her for the risks she had taken—both in freeing him and in relying on her judgment that he was what he claimed to be. If he had been a CR man, he could have caught or killed her at any time after she had rescued him.

He said, "Why did you do all this? Why should you think so much of me?"

"Not of you," she said. "But of Tim Killian. And of my people. If what you said is true—if he is wounded—I may need your help. And then there was the plan, to free the *abuela* and the *tía*."

Marne grinned a little at being put so bluntly in his place. "I'm the man I claim to be," he said. "And we'll help your grandmother and aunt—and anyone else who's held at the CR."

He drew the dun back from the waterhole. "How far is it to Killian's camp?"

"Perhaps a half hour if we ride steadily," she said. She mounted and looked down at him. "You have not yet told me what that man Carnap meant when he told the other man not to hit you."

Marne climbed aboard the dun and followed Marita up the sandy trail. "I didn't know myself until after they caught me," he said. He grimaced as he thought of the ease of that capture. "They had me boxed in—cliffs on one side of the road, a steep pitch on the other, and two guards waiting up ahead. I didn't stand a chance."

"You did not try to fight them?"

"Not with those odds," he said. "I thought I'd have a better chance later. Besides, I wouldn't have minded going to the CR. I'd like to snoop around there a bit."

"Looking for what?"

He stared at her. She twisted about, facing him. "Tim— Lieutenant Killian didn't tell you?"

"He said he was hunting Carnap and Doncaster. That is all."

"You might as well know the truth now," he decided. Briefly, he explained Doncaster's purpose and what Killian had learned, what the provost-marshal's office suspected.

She said accusingly, "Then you are still in the army! You lied!"

"What would you have done if I hadn't?" he demanded. "To your people an army man represented the Mexican government. Before that, he stood for Spain. That meant a disregard for your personal rights. The army took your money in taxes. It took your food. It used your homes. It helped itself to the women of the village. These are things you and Tonio have never experienced, but I'm sure you heard about them from the time you were small children."

"It is so," she agreed. "It is the story that Doncaster told my people. He said the American army was even worse than the Mexican army had been many years before. Some of us knew it was a lie, but we could not make the old ones believe."

Her voice sharpened. "But that is not why Tonio and I fear your army, nor why the *abuelo* fears it. We are afraid because if you should bring troops before our people are taken from the CR, they will be killed."

"I know that," Marne said. He smiled a little. "It's a good thing you and Killian, ah, feel the way you do about one another or he might not be alive now."

It was her turn to smile. She blushed slightly and turned away. They rode on for another quarter of a mile. She turned suddenly, but this time she held the .38 she carried in her holster. She aimed it steadily at him.

"You will drop your guns carefully to the ground," she ordered.

Marne gaped at her. She went on, "We are very close to the camp. I cannot take any chances."

"In other words, you still don't trust me to be the man I say I am?"

"You have not yet explained those words Tonio heard," she said. "Why is that?" She added swiftly, "I wish to trust you. I need your help. But if I am wrong, then I will have killed Tim. Drop your guns, Señor Marne."

"What if Doncaster's men have found the camp and are waiting?"

She said, "That is the risk we must take."

Her expression told him that she would shoot if he didn't obey her order. Carefully, he drew his .44 and let it fall to the sand. His carbine followed. Then, on her command, he backed the dun away long enough for her to get both guns. Once more back in the saddle, she motioned him to go ahead.

"I am still waiting for the explanation," she said.

Marne touched the dun's flanks with his heels, sending it walking forward. "As I understand from what Carnap said to the guards, Doncaster couldn't figure out who I was or what I was up to. He wanted to find out—before he killed me."

He turned, grinning at her. "When a man's as close to success as Doncaster thinks he is—when the long wait's about over—then he starts worrying. The pressures are on him. Everything makes him nervous. And when a man is nervous, he tends to make mistakes. That's our big hope—to force him into making a mistake."

She listened without comment or change of expression. Then she said, "It is around the sharp bend ahead. He will see you before you see him."

"If he's there to see us," Marne said.

"Let us hope he looks first," Marita murmured. "He will expect only Tonio or me. If he does not recognize you at once, Señor Marne, he may shoot."

Knowing Killian and what he had been through recently,

Marne had to agree with her. And, he thought, the Lieutenant wouldn't be looking for him. He'd expect Marne by now to be back at the Fort.

Taking a deep breath, Marne sent the dun around the bend and into the open.

XIV

KILLIAN'S CAMP lay squeezed against a canyon wall under a canopy of rock. The canyon widened here to a full hundred feet. When Marne swept around the bend in the trail, he was looking for the overhang. But the distance between the trail on the far right and the camp on the far left was cluttered with willows and scrub timber, forming an effective screen.

Marne slowed the dun and stood up in the stirrups. He was drawing in a deep breath to call Killian's name when the gunshot sent him down and forward over the horse's neck.

"It's Marne!" he shouted.

The shot had come through the screen of trees and he turned his head and looked in that direction. Only a thin wisp of smoke rising in the air told of anyone's presence. Otherwise, there was no sign of life that Marne could see. It was as if the gun blast had momentarily quieted the insect noises, the quick chirping of the mountain birds, even the rustle of the light breeze through the tree branches.

"Lieutenant!" Marne called in a parade ground bellow.

"Come in with your hands reaching," a voice answered. It was Killian talking, Marne was sure. But there was a slurred sound to the words, a thickness that made the tone difficult to pin down exactly.

Marne lifted his arms, holding the reins high, and started the dun to the left. He heard the hoofbeats coming lightly behind him and turned to see Marita rounding the bend.

She still held her gun on him, and the expression on her face showed more doubt about him than he had seen before. But then, Killian's answer hadn't been the kind to make her believe Marne.

Steering the horse with his knees, Marne let it poke its way through the willows, across a rock-strewn dry creek bed, and up a low bank to another stand of willows. Killian's thin line of gunsmoke had given Marne his location, but here in the trees he found he was no longer sure of the exact direction and again he called out:

"Lieutenant."

"Keep riding straight ahead."

The voice was closer and the slurred speech, the thickness of voice were more pronounced. Marne urged the dun on. Past the second line of willows, a flat stretch of sand extended to the bank that was covered by the rock canopy. Now Marne could see Killian's small camp—the few pieces of gear neatly in place, a dry stick fire laid and waiting for a match, the horse tethered in a small grassy spot to one side. But there was no sign of Tim Killian himself.

"Lieutenant!" Marne snapped again.

The voice came from the back of the overhang, where deep shadow squeezed out all light. "Keep your hands high."

Marne remained where he was. He heard Marita bring her horse almost alongside the dun, but neither of them spoke. Then Killian appeared. Marne caught Marita's gasp, and he choked back a desire to curse out his surprise.

Killian was walking with the aid of a cut willow sapling for a crutch. He held his .44 almost laxly in his right hand, as though he lacked the strength to grip it tightly. He moved slowly, with an obvious limp and in obvious pain. But it was his face that held Marne's gaze. His weather darkened skin looked as if it had been drained of blood, of life. His eyes stared out from under the shadow of his hat brim wild and feverish. And even from where Marne sat, he could see the ravages of the fever on Killian's mouth.

Is he going to know me at all? Marne wondered. He made a move to get off the horse. Killian was leaning forward as if trying to see him more clearly. As Marne stirred, he slowly brought his gun up.

Marne said, "There's another gun on me back here. You don't have to worry."

"Who's with you?"

"Marita Farrel."

Killian said, "Marita . . . ?" as if he were sending the name far off to find and bring back the mental picture connected with it.

Again Marne heard Marita's gasp. Without looking at her, he said, "He needs help. You can keep your gun on me if you want. I'm going to him."

He dropped to the ground and strode forward. His eyes were fixed on Killian's gun hand. But it did not move any farther upward. Killian remained with his body bent forward, his gaze aimed at Marne's approaching figure. Behind him, Marne heard Marita leave her sorrel and start quickly forward. He knew without bothering to turn that she would still be holding her .38 on his back.

He was within three feet of Killian before the slurred voice came again. "Captain Marne! I thought you'd gone back . . ." He broke off. "Sir, I want . . ." A second time he stopped. Marne stepped quickly forward, catching Killian as he sagged forward.

Marita murmured, *"Madre de Dios,"* and dropped to her knees as Marne laid Killian carefully on the packed sand beneath the overhanging canopy of rock.

Marne came down beside her. "It's his hip," he said. "That's where the bullet scoured him." He pointed to where Killian had cut away part of his trousers and wadded a bandage made from part of his shirt against the flesh, lashing it to himself with piggin strings.

She touched Killian's gaunt cheek and rolled back an eyelid with a practiced thumb. "He is still very strong," she said in a relieved voice. "The fever has not been with him very long."

"Even so, we'd better get at that wound," Marne said. He glanced up at her. "If you can trust me to help."

She said without apology, "I did what I had to do. I would have been a fool to accept you completely without proof."

Marne nodded. "Can we build a fire?" He gestured at the pile of dry sticks. "Where does the smoke go? I don't want to lead CR men here. They're sure to be hunting Killian even now."

"Tonio chose this place because it is safe to build a fire," she said. She pointed to the rear of the overhang. "Back there a slit on the rock takes the smoke far away before it comes above the ground."

"Let's boil some water then," Marne said. He rose. "I've got some medicine in my saddle bags. If you can find some clean cloth, we can put a decent bandage on."

Marita went to her pack and brought back a clean linen underskirt. While Marne lit the fire and set water on to heat, she tore the cloth into strips. Then she examined the few medicines Marne had laid out.

She was about to speak when Marne swore sharply. She turned. He was kneeling beside Killian. He had cut away the rough bandage and was staring at the bullet mangled hip.

"The shot missed the bone," Marne said, "but it took a hunk of meat away with it." He grunted. "It festered up fast. I wonder why he didn't clean it out in time?"

"Perhaps he was running from them until a few hours ago," she suggested.

"It happened almost forty-eight hours ago," Marne said. Rising, he went to get the steaming water and the medicines. He was about to begin washing the wound when Marita said gently, "Let me," and moved in front of him.

She worked with delicate but sure strokes of her hands, quickly in case Killian should regain consciousness while his wound lay open, exposed to the air. By the time she and Marne were affixing the clean bandages, Killian's eyelids were beginning to twitch.

"You did that like an expert," Marne said.

90

Her smile touched him warmly. "I learned in St. Louis. But I never did this for anyone so—so important before."

Killian's eyes came open. The short period of unconsciousness had obviously been like a sleep to him. His eyes were clearer and his voice less thick. "Marita!"

Marne rose and stepped back as they looked at one another. They had no need of words between them, he saw, and briefly he envied a man whose woman would look at him this way.

Marita moved away suddenly. "What did you eat last?" she demanded.

Killian grimaced. His eyes slid past her and rested on Marne. "Captain Marne!"

Marita and Marne looked at one another, both realizing that Killian had no memory of what had taken place a short while before. Marne said, "I didn't get back to the fort, Lieutenant. But what about it—when did you eat last?"

Killian wiped his forehead with the back of his hand. "The night before that day you helped me—whenever that was," he said. "I think I recall finding a few berries last night—or maybe it was night before last—but they didn't fill me much."

Marne said, "Of course. Your food would be in the saddlebags on the horse Tink and Smitty shot out from under you. Marita . . ."

But she was already bringing food from her pack and carrying it toward the fire. She had an earthen jar and two wrapped packages. From the jar she poured what was unmistakeably chicken soup into a camp pan. In a few minutes the odor drifted toward Marne and Killian. One of the packages yielded tortillas, which she heated. The other contained coffee.

Marne let Killian rest while the food was being prepared. After a drink from Marne's bottle of whiskey, he was able to sit up propped against the side of the overhang. He ate his soup ravenously, mopping the pan with pieces of tortilla. Borrowing Marne's tobacco, he stuffed his pipe and leaned his head back, his coffee resting beside him.

"I think I'll live," he said. His smile touched Marita. Then it faded as he glanced at Marne. "Now, sir, I want to report."

Marita had dug more food from her pack. Now she offered Marne a plate of beans and some tortillas. He began to eat. "Go ahead, Lieutenant."

Marita said, "You called the Señor Marne 'Captain.' He is your officer then?" She sounded as if she thought their positions should be reversed.

"Captain Marne," Killian said. His voice was clear, almost strong now. The fevered glow was nearly gone from his eyes. "The best rebel hunter in the west."

"I have seen him fight," she said. "I am glad he is your friend."

Killian said to Marne, "After I got away up there on the bench, I figured the last place any CR man would look for me would be close to the ranch. So I went there and hid. I couldn't hear or see much but Doncaster and Rutter did a lot of ordering and had most of the crew out looking for me. I took advantage and spent the night and some of the next morning checking out those big barns I told you about."

Marne swallowed a mouthful of beans. "And you found what we expected?"

"And more," Killian said heavily. "They must have been collecting guns and ammunition and other goods for years, sir. I even found a batch of cavalry uniforms, all baled up like cotton ready for shipping."

"Uniforms!" Marne whispered. He said loudly, "If they dressed a crew of men in cavalry clothes and then started raiding . . ."

Killian nodded. Words weren't necessary to picture the panic the settlers would be in. And once burned, they wouldn't know when to trust a uniform. They would have no way of knowing which uniformed men were genuine, which false.

"Staple foods, wagons being readied and loaded—everything Doncaster needs to make his hit," Killian went on. "And from the looks of things, he's about ready."

Marne said, "The information is important, but letting your wound go while you got it was a fool thing to do."

"So I found out," Killian said. "I was hungry and getting feverish and I tried to sneak to where I could get my hands on some food. But I wasn't thinking very clearly, I guess. I almost got caught. I had to ride for it again. I remember turning down the trail that would take me here. Then I don't recall anything clearly again until I saw you and Marita a while ago."

He gulped his coffee. "I saw Marita's people. They're still all right."

Marne was filling his pipe. He said slowly, "There's not much we can do until we get them out." He looked up, a lopsided grin tugging at the edges of his mouth. "And this might be the best time. With the CR hunting both of us, they might not have too many hands around the place."

Killian sat up straight. "Tonight about dark, we can . . ."

"Not 'we,' " Marne snapped. "You're on sick call right now, Lieutenant. I'll do what's necessary." He turned to Marita. "He can't ride yet, but do you think you can leave him long enough to get to town and bring back some food? I imagine your people will be hungry after they've been here a while."

"Here?" She stared at him.

"Can you think of a safer place for me to bring them?" Marne asked.

She nodded, understanding brightening her eyes. Then she frowned. "But how can you do this? Always they are guarded. Doncaster knows having the *abuelo* and the *tía* and the others is the only way he can control my people." The brightness left her eyes as fear shadowed her face.

"You know what kind of man Doncaster is," she said. "And Rutter. If they think their safety is threatened, they will kill . . ." She broke off and then repeated, "How can you do this?"

"I don't know yet," Marne admitted. "But it has to be done. It's the only thing that will give us a chance to stop them. We have to get your people safely away before we can risk a move."

He started away and turned. "I haven't any ideas now, but I'll think of one by the time I get to the CR." Reaching the dun, he lifted himself into the saddle. Touching his fingers to the brim of his hat, he reined the horse around and rode slowly away.

XV

TONIO STIRRED restlessly on the narrow cot where he had fallen asleep some time before. He had no way of knowing whether it was daytime or night, or just how much time had passed since Elena had finished treating his wound and helped Pablo bring him here. The room where he lay was a basement alcove, around a corner from the shadowy wine cellar. A candle gave a little light; beyond it there was only thick darkness.

He looked down at his bandaged leg and swore softly. Marita and her foolishness! As if he was not man enough to ignore a scratch such as this one! Was he expected to lie here like a frightened old woman because of it, and because men from the CR were hunting him?

He sat up, swung his legs carefully to the floor, and even more carefully made an effort to stand. He could feel the beginning of pain as his weight came onto his bandaged leg. But the sensation grew no stronger and he took a tentative step. His face split into a grin of pride. He limped a bit, true, but what difference would that make once he was on horseback?

And he must find a horse quickly. He had work to do. Marita might think that all of her troubles would be solved when she found Tim Killian, but he, Tonio, knew better. She was a woman in love and she did not think clearly. The thought of what could happen if a wounded Tim Killian and Marita tried to do something on their own frightened Tonio.

He had a desire to rush out, to mount his horse and ride.

He forced himself to calmness. His wound was slight but still he would be wiser to have some help, to find someone who would be able to make Marita be sensible. The *abuelo*, of course.

Tonio limped to the foot of the stone steps leading up from the basement. He called Pablo softly, hoping that no CR man might be in hearing distance. A door opened and shut and footsteps started down toward him. Tonio drew back into shadow and waited, his eyes on the foot of the stairs.

Pablo appeared. He was an old man, stooped and wrinkled, but he moved briskly enough. And his voice was strong when he swore at seeing Tonio out of bed.

"*Basta*," Tonio said quickly. "Enough, *amigo*. I must talk to the *abuelo* at once. And I will need a pair of trousers."

He saw the stubbornness settle on the old man's face and he added quickly, "Marita has gone off to help the man who was here before—Killian. But the new one who came yesterday, he wants to find Killian too. He will follow her and kill them both. Now hurry!"

The old man's expression said that he did not understand all of this. But he did understand the threat to his Marita. Quickly, he turned and hurried up the stairs. Tonio returned to his cot and lay waiting impatiently.

His grandfather and the trousers arrived at the same time. While he dressed, Tonio told the sheriff what had happened and explained his suspicion of Marne.

"I could not feel that about him," the sheriff said. "He has not the—the way of a man who would lie this way."

Tonio's impatience prodded him close to rudeness. "What does it matter? Even if I am wrong, Marita has gone to find Tim Killian. What if the CR discovers her there? And if I am right, she is in danger from this Marne also."

The sheriff thought of his impetuous granddaughter. "*Sí*, he said. "I will go."

To Tonio's surprise, he did not have to argue the sheriff into letting him go along. Watching him walk, his grandfather said, "You will be all right as long as you are on your horse."

With a fresh bay pony under him, Tonio began to feel better. The sheriff rode a leggy paint with just enough white showing for Tonio to make it out in the darkness that was gathering in the valley.

"CR men have been moving through town and, some of the men say, along the trails," the sheriff told Tonio. "But there are none in town right now."

"Once we are on the trail to take us to Marita, they will not find us," Tonio said. "They do not know of it."

"We are not going to find this Killian's hiding place," the sheriff said flatly. "Marita and he will no longer be there." He turned a grim mask toward Tonio. "You know your cousin, *chico*. She and the man will go to the CR. You heard her talk of her plan before. She has some crazy idea that she can save the *abuela* and . . ."

He was right, Tonio thought. While he had slept Marita would have reached Tim Killian. And if he was not too badly wounded, they would have left the hiding place—to escape Marne. And where else would a foolish one like Marita go but to the rancho?

"I know a back trail . . ." Tonio began.

"You would teach me to suck eggs?" the sheriff demanded. "There are many back trails. I knew them before you were born." He started his horse into the darkness. With a grimace, Tonio followed.

Killian watched the darkness slide down into the canyon. Marita lay near by, breathing softly and evenly in her sleep. She had deliberately sought some rest once she was sure he would be all right. "In case your friend does bring back the *abuela* and the others," she had explained. "When I awake, I will go for the food."

At first Killian had wanted her to stay awake, to tell him what had happened the past two days, to explain why she had acted toward Marne as she had—friendly, but not really outgoing, and at times almost apologetic. But Marita had told him to wait, that she would explain when he was rested.

Now he was glad she had fallen asleep. The thought of Marne trying to slip into the CR by himself worried Killian. He had done it, yes. But he had had time to examine the place, to know its strengths and weaknesses. Marne had never seen it before.

Killian rose slowly to his feet. He stood motionless while a wave of dizziness passed. Then he walked quietly and steadily away from the campfire. He stopped by his gear and buckled on his gunbelt. Slipping his arm under his saddle, he heaved it up to his shoulder. The weight threatened to send him to the ground as solid pain coursed through his hip, but he fought it grimly and in a moment was able to walk again.

Locating his horse, he saddled it and, with an effort, pulled himself aboard. He rose to where he could see the camp. Marita still lay sleeping, obviously exhausted from the nervous strain of the day's happenings.

It was in his mind that he had to find help for Marne. And he could think of only one place to go—Arroyo Verde. There he could get Tonio. The boy had a quick mind. Between them, they should be able to figure out something to do.

Killian backtracked along the trail Marita and Marne had followed to reach his camp. As he reached the point where he would ride to the junction of the two gullies, he heard horses, and he pulled up his mount. The sounds lessened and he rode carefully into the open. He could see two riders dimly as he looked in the direction of the CR. They were following a rise and suddenly both were outlined against the night sky. Killian had been about to turn in the opposite direction, but now he reined his horse back.

Those weren't CR men, he thought. Not unless they'd taken to wearing the broad-brimmed, high crowned hats the local *vaqueros* all wore. He leaned forward, straining his eyes as if he might be able to recognize one of the men. But they dipped out of sight and he settled back in the saddle.

"Nothing to do but follow," he said to the horse. If those were townsmen up ahead, that meant something was in the wind. Killian could think of no other reason for any of them to be riding to the CR by this back trail.

He trailed quietly, staying far enough back to keep from being heard. Twice he glimpsed them. Then the contours of the land hid them from his view. Finally he topped the last rise and stopped to look down a rolling slope toward a scatter of trees. Through the trees, lights from the CR ranchhouse made yellow pinpricks in the night. As he watched someone passed between him and the lights. A second form blocked the tiny bright spots. Both riders were down there, then. Killian urged his horse down the slope.

He was almost to the trees, the point where he planned to leave the horse and go on foot, when the click of a gun hammer being drawn back froze him in the saddle.

A voice said softly, "Ride very slowly, señor. Manos arriba!"

Killian said in a relieved tone, "It's me, Killian, Tonio," but he lifted his hands as he had been commanded.

"Ay, Tim!" Tonio rode forward. His grandfather moved up beside him. "What has happened? Where is Marita? Why is she not with you?"

Killian said quickly, in an effort to stem the excited flood of questions, "She and Marne came to my camp. She's resting there. I came to get help . . ."

"And Marne?" Tonio demanded in a hoarse whisper. "What of him?"

"That's why I came for help," Killian answered. "He came here. He's looking for your people."

"You see!" Tonio cried in Spanish. "What did I tell you?" He swung his horse around and lashed his heels into its flanks. Before Killian or the sheriff could move, he sent the bay surging through the trees.

"Madre de Dios!" Potrero gasped. "He is riding for the house. He will have everyone killed!"

98

XVI

IT WAS WELL into the afternoon when Marne rode away
from Killian's camp. He kept a slow pace, walking the dun
back along the trail Marita had brought him here by. Shortly
before he reached the point where this hidden trail came
more into the open, he stopped and carefully checked over
his guns.

Dusk was slipping down as he rode cautiously into the
junction of the two gullies. He studied the trails but saw no
sign of any movement. Stilling the dun, he held his breath
and listened. But if a rider was within earshot, he moved too
quietly for Marne's sharp hearing. Satisfied, he turned in the
direction Carnap and Fitz had been taking him when Marita
had attacked. This was not a part of the Diablos familiar to
Marne, but he had no doubts about following this twisting
up and down route. It could lead to only one place.

And then suddenly the CR was there. Marne reined in the
dun. He stared down a rolling slope and through a scatter of
trees at the bulk of a number of buildings looming blackly
in the early darkness. Light came from the building farthest
up the slope, and he knew it would be the ranch house.

He rode on, stepping the horse lightly to the edge of the
trees. Here Marne slid to the ground. He tied the dun and
then moved about through the trees, orienting himself. Once
he was sure that he could find his way about this unfamiliar
terrain, he led the dun to a spot well away from the trail
but not far behind the rear of the house. Tying it, he walked
softly away.

Those bulky masses against the night would be the barns,
he judged, and the long, narrow building to one side of the
house would be the bunkhouse. It sat dark and silent as if
it might be empty at this time of evening. But Marne thought
of this as a miniature army camp rather than a ranch, and

he guessed that night shift guards could well be sleeping in there.

Softly he followed the slope of the hill, making a wide arc around the rear of the house and coming against the bunkhouse wall at the far side. The building was well made, without any cracks between the boards, and he realized that he would have to go to the door if he wanted to hear any sounds from inside.

He reached the front corner of the building and paused. The night was dark, moonless, as it would be for some time yet. The only light except the thin cold glitter of the stars came from the big house itself. A half dozen windows in various rooms were lighted, spraying their yellow glow out onto the dirt of the yard. Around Marne, night animals rustled in the grass and large, horny-shelled beetles made clicking sounds as they flew against the closed lighted windows. In the distance a coyote complained and another sympathized with it. Well up in the high country a mountain lion sent its sobbing cry drifting faintly down. Distant though the sound might be, it stirred the horses in the corral, adding their fretting to the restless night.

To Marne, trying to listen for telltale footsteps, the various noises combined into a discordant symphony. Then with startling suddenness, there was a long moment of quiet. He had moved close to the bunkhouse door and now he eased it open a crack and leaned forward. The air that reached him from inside had the familiar odor of a barracks about it—a mixture of unwashed bodies and clothes, of unopened windows, of gun oil and tobacco smoke.

He caught only the scents; no sounds accompanied them. As far as he could judge, the bunkhouse was empty. Marne backed away, latching the door quietly. The cougar cried again and once more the cacophony arose. Marne pressed in shadow against the bunkhouse wall and planned his next move.

This close to the enemy, the sense of danger rode strongly through him, and his mouth quirked upward in its tight, anticipatory grin. His hands ached with a desire to get Doncaster in their grip, but Marne thrust the feeling aside. His job now was to pull the CR's teeth—to get Marita's relatives away. Once he managed that, then he would have the whole of Arroyo Verde behind him. Then Doncaster's formidable force of gunhands would have little meaning.

But where to look? The kitchen, at this time of night, he decided. Someone passed back and forth across two lighted windows set side by side. A thin line of smoke rose from the roof above the windows. To one side of them was the darkened outline of a rear veranda. Those lights had to come from a kitchen, then.

He stepped quietly forward, walking openly but without haste toward the lights. Near their outer edge, he stopped and made a wide swing that brought him against the house well with the lighted windows between him and the dark veranda. Now he eased forward along the wall until he was under the nearer window. Taking off his hat, he straightened carefully until his eyes were above the sill. Only a thin curtain separated him from a clear view of the interior.

Marne's grin broadened and his eyes glittered with pleasure. Inside, at a long deal table, six people were eating supper. One was obviously the ranch cook—he looked like a hundred other cooks Marne had seen in army camps throughout the west. A second was just as obviously a guard. He sat away from the others, his eyes never still, and his gun hanging openly at his side even while he ate.

The other four were the ones that interested Marne. Two were women, and he thought he would have recognized them anywhere. The older was slender with strands of gray in still dark hair. Her face was lined with weariness but it had not yet blotted out the almost arrogant beauty of her features. This would be Marita's grandmother. The other woman was younger, a bit more plump but still obviously the older one's daughter. Marita and Tonio's aunt. And the two boys, perhaps fifteen and sixteen, would be the younger woman's sons. They were like Tonio with their sharp, cleanly chiseled features, their olive skin and black hair; and with the smoldering anger showing in their eyes.

Marne thought, *I'll have to get four horses saddled and put them close by*. The boys could fight, of course, if he could get weapons to them. The women probably could too. He didn't doubt but that they had used guns more than once during their lives in this still raw country.

First the horses. Then the guns. He dropped below the window sill and moved toward the rear veranda. When he was well away from the edge of the glow from the windows, he stepped into the yard, toward the barn that had the corral attached.

He was less than a half dozen strides from the rear steps, and on a direct line with the door, when light slashed out, catching him squarely. Marne turned, his hand slapping for his gun. The door had been opened. A man was framed in it, and the light glinted on the rifle he held. It was aimed directly at Marne.

"Hold still." The voice was level, almost pleasantly conversational, and now Marne saw that it was Doncaster. "There's a man behind you and one posted at each corner of the yard." Mockery tinged his words. "You haven't any place to go this time."

Marne held his hands away from his sides and started forward as the rifle barrel moved, beckoning him. He started to curse his own carelessness and stopped. What carelessness? he wondered. These men had not surrounded him by chance. They had known he was here and had moved as quietly as he, getting to their positions. In some way that he could not fathom, they had been warned of his coming.

Doncaster backed away as Marne stepped into the house. He was at one end of the kitchen with the six at the table on his left. He glanced that way and saw the four Spanish-Americans look quickly at him and away.

"These are the people you came for?" Doncaster murmured.

Marne looked blank. "People?" He shook his head. "I came to see you." He thrust his head forward. "That is, if you're the one called Doncaster."

"Didn't they tell you at the posada who I am?"

Marne let his body drop into a slight slouch. "They told me a lot of things—that the one I whipped wanted to kill me, among other pieces of news." The sarcasm in his voice as he said 'news' made Doncaster's lips lift in a smile.

"Follow me," he said abruptly. Turning, he led the way down a hall and into a large, airy parlor. A series of lamps gave a strong light and a fire in the large stone fireplace threw out the warmth needed to take away the chill of a mountain night. It was the kind of room Marne associated with a man like Doncaster.

Doncaster dropped into a comfortable chair, keeping the rifle close to hand. He motioned for Marne to sit down on the big couch.

"Now," Doncaster said, "let me hear the rest of this story of yours." His mouth framed amusement as he studied Marne. "The account I heard from Carnap doesn't make you sound like even a good liar."

Marne said, "I told Carnap I wanted to see you. He was bringing me here when that fool girl jumped us."

"But you went off with her."

"With my hands tied and a gun at my back, what was I supposed to do?" Marne demanded.

Doncaster's look became more thoughtful. "Carnap claims you and that boy were trying to sneak away when he caught you. The boy killed one of my men."

Marne let Doncaster see his smile. "If Carnap hadn't bumbled in when he did, I'd have had a prize for you." He leaned back, taking out his pipe and pouch. He filled the pipe as he talked.

"The story I got in Arroyo Verde was that you're looking for an army man by the name of Killian. He's supposed to be hiding somewhere in these mountains."

Doncaster nodded briefly. Marne paused to light his pipe and then went on, "I also got the impression that Tonio and the girl knew where this Killian might be. So I worked them around until they agreed to take me to him."

"Why should they do that?"

"They want him out of the Diablos, but he's supposed to

be shot up. I said I knew a way out and I could pack him, shot up or not."

Doncaster remained expressionless. "Go on."

"That's all. I was following the kid when that fool Carnap had to come in like a Saturday night drunk shooting up the town."

"And just why should you find this Killian for me?"

"Why?" Marne blew a thin cloud of smoke. "I need a job. I need money. I've been in Mexico too long, making too little *dinero.* I heard that someone up here was paying good wages with prospects for more if a man turned out worth his hire. So I came."

"And introduced yourself by running two of my men into jail," Doncaster said.

"I have one talent to sell," Marne said. "My guess is that a man like you will pay a fancy price for something worth having. I was giving you a sample."

Doncaster threw back his head and laughed. The sound died abruptly as Rutter came into the room. "Well?"

"We found his horse. Nothing else. It looks like he's alone."

His face still showed the effects of his fight with Marne. He stood in a doorway, his expression sullen and hating as he looked at Marne.

"Did you fix the alarm?"

"We couldn't find the thread in the dark. I told Carnap and Fitz to wait until morning. Some of the crews'll be back in soon. They can stand guard."

Doncaster turned to Marne. "The instant you left the trail and started through the trees, an ingenious device of mine warned us of your presence."

"I wondered," Marne said. "I moved too quiet for you to hear me."

"Loves himself, don't he," Rutter commented sourly.

Marne glanced at him. "Some of us have reason to love ourselves. Others don't."

Rutter swore and started forward. Doncaster cut off his movement with a lift of his hand. He said to Marne, "A fine

104

linen thread is run through the trees breast high to a horse. Most animals who wander through those trees would pass under the thread. A man or his mount would not. You hit the thread and broke it, probably thinking it was a twig in your way—if you noticed it at all."

"I didn't."

"Good. To go on—the thread is attached near the house to a heavier cord. When the thread breaks, the cord sags by its own weight. Attached to the far end of the cord—inside the house—is a small bell. The sag of the cord set the bell ringing. I knew the instant you started down through the trees."

He spoke, Marne thought, almost like one of the lecturers at West Point. At the same time he was as pleasant as a fellow officer relaxing off duty. But Marne knew how much of a mask this facade could be. He knew just how vicious Doncaster could turn. How cold the smiling eyes could become, how thin and hard the pleasant mouth.

He said carefully, "We're even. I made fools of your men. You caught me. Now let's get to business."

"*We* ain't even," Rutter growled. He took another step forward. "I didn't finish with you yet."

Marne stood up. "Any time," he said softly. He smiled. "First I'll whip you and then I'll take your job. I'm better fit for it anyway."

Doncaster laughed suddenly. The sound seemed to goad Rutter. He lunged at Marne, pawing for his gun.

Marne had a glimpse of Doncaster reaching for his rifle, and he knew that if he drew on Rutter, he would be gunned down. He was an unknown quantity to Doncaster; he was expendable.

Marne took two swift strides forward. Rutter had his gun barrel clear of leather when Marne reached him. Rutter threw up his left arm and leaned to one side as Marne feinted a hard fist at his face. Laughing, Marne stepped around behind Rutter and caught his gun arm. He jerked savagely, sending Rutter's gun flying to land across the room. Without seeming to pause, Marne brought Rutter's arm up behind his back. Rutter howled his anger and pain.

"That's enough!" Doncaster snapped. "There'll be enough fighting for this organization without you doing it to each other."

"What is he around here?" Rutter demanded truculently.

"I don't know yet," Doncaster murmured. He still held his rifle in such a way that he could lift the barrel and fire easily. His eyes were speculatively on Marne. They remained on him.

"I can't find nobody . . ." a voice began from the doorway. It stopped abruptly. Marne turned to see Carnap standing there, staring at him. "By God, it's the joker I caught today!"

"The one who let you catch him," Marne said smoothly. He was grinning again but not at the threat from Rutter's antagonism or Doncaster's caution. He was thinking of the danger that Carnap represented. He was the one man who could identify Marne for what he was. If he should make the wrong move, say the wrong thing . . .

It was too late, he realized. Recognition was blossoming on Carnap's face. "That voice!" he cried. "It's been plaguing me all day. Now I remember." He swung to Doncaster. "This is the joker that had me locked up that night in Arizona. He's the army man we set the trap for!"

Marne saw Doncaster's surprise turn to grudging admiration and then icy amusement. His rifle barrel lifted. Rutter strode across the room to his gun. Before he reached it, Carnap had his .44 in his hand.

A shot crashing outside swung Rutter and Carnap toward the windows. Only Doncaster remained as he was, his rifle held on Marne. A second gunshot came and a man cursed in a thin voice.

"That's Fitz!" Carnap cried.

"Go see to him." Doncaster continued to look at Marne.

As Carnap turned the front door crashed open. Footsteps hammered down the hall, and Carnap was suddenly spun back into the parlor, driven by a wild rush from Tonio.

For a long instant, the boy stood in the doorway, panting.

His eyes fixed themselves on Marne. He shouted, *"Traidor! Engañador!"*

His gun came up and he fired.

XVII

THE WILDNESS IN Tonio's expression told Marne more than his accusing cry of "Traitor! Trickster!" As the boy's gun came up, Marne took the only chance he had. He leaped onto the sofa and dived for cover behind its high back.

As he moved, Doncaster brought up his rifle and fired. The bullet whispered past Marne's disappearing body and ripped out through a window. Now Rutter and Carnap were shooting, their lead ripping into the heavy padding of the sofa back.

Marne shouted to Tonio in Spanish, "Get out of here, you fool, before they kill you too! And take your people with you. They're in the kitchen." Complete silence answered him.

Lifting his .44 from his holster, he bellied down on the floor and peered through the narrow space between the pegged wooden floorboards and the sagging bottom of the sofa. Boots came into view as someone moved with an attempt at quiet. Other boots showed in the opposite direction.

Marne grinned savagely. They were trying to flank him, to get to the end of the sofa where they could draw their beads. But this huge piece of furniture was a miniature fortress. It stood out from the wall and the windows a good four feet. Its back rose high enough to protect Marne even if he rose to his knees. And the stuffing sucked up lead the way soft paper sucked up water.

Doncaster said suddenly, "Where the devil is that kid? One of you go after him. And see to Fitz. You, Carnap. Rutter and I can handle the army man."

Marne called lightly, "The name is Marne, Doncaster. Captain Curtis Marne, attached to the Provost-Marshal's office. I'm the man who's been dogging you for two years."

"That will give me even more satisfaction—when I kill you," Doncaster answered thinly.

Marne saw one pair of boots move quickly to the door and disappear. Those would belong to Carnap. Then the unpolished ones still easing toward the far end of the couch would be Rutter's. That left the shiny pair for Doncaster. They were coming straight ahead.

Marne glanced behind him, at the window. How long before Doncaster thought of going out and shooting at him from there? Or how long before the search crews would start drifting back? Once that happened, Doncaster would have a dozen men where he now had only a few.

He needed room to maneuver, Marne decided. As strong as his position was at the moment, he couldn't hope to stay here for long. Carefully, he aimed through the small space between the floor and the bottom of the couch. He fired, deliberately sending his bullet splintering wood close to Rutter's feet.

Rutter cursed and leaped up and backwards. Marne called, "The next time I'll splinter your ankle bone. Now get back across the room—both of you!"

Rutter hesitated, but finally he moved back. After a long moment of hesitation, Doncaster followed suit. Again, Marne turned and studied the bullet-shattered window behind him.

He thought, "One good leap . . ." If he moved fast enough to avoid being shot and if he landed without knocking out his wind, he would have a chance of finding safety in the darkness only a few feet away. Then he could get to the rear and help Tonio.

Before Marne could act, a gun shattered the quiet. It came from the rear of the house. A second shot and a third. Tonio's voice rose in a shrill Spanish curse filled with pain.

Marne waited no longer. He turned, poised, and thrust himself upward. His hat crashed through the already broken glass. He felt sharp shards slash at his shoulders. Behind him two guns roared. A bullet whipped at his heel. Another whistled past and into the night. He felt himself falling and then, abruptly, the hard boards of the veranda slapped up at him.

Marne rolled, the way he would land if he had been pitched from a horse. He came to his feet, staggered, caught his balance, and plunged toward the end of the veranda. The moon was topping the mountain rim now and the faint light showed him the railing. Feet hammered as someone ran onto the veranda. Marne leaped onto the railing and jumped down into the darkness below it.

His feet hit dirt and he ran, turning the corner of the house and sprinting for the rear. A shadow loomed up ahead, coming down from the trees on the slope behind the house. Marne lifted his gun. He let it drop as Sheriff Potrero stepped into thin rays of moonlight.

Marne called softly in Spanish, "Help me. Tonio's in there trying to bring your people out."

"Marne?"

A gun tore apart the night with a gout of flame. It came from behind Marne. Lead ripped at the dirt close to his feet. He ran for the protection of the house corner. The sheriff answered the shot and then stumbled to safety beside him.

"That fool boy thinks you are a traitor . . ."

"I know," Marne interrupted. "Forget it. He needs help. We have to get him and your people out of there. We need horses." He broke off, his head cocked as he listened for sounds that would tell him what was happening. But the night was strangely still. There seemed to be no movement—outside or in the house.

"Killian has the horses," the sheriff whispered. "He has five extra ones, including your own. He will bring them at a signal."

Marne didn't wait to question Killian's presence here. From almost directly behind him, on the other side of the house wall, someone fired twice rapidly. A different gun answered. A third sounded. Someone cried out.

Marne raced for the rear door. "Stand guard!" he called to Potrero. His feet found the steps. He crossed the narrow veranda and jerked open the door. The kitchen was in darkness, but light came from beneath a closed door to the left. Marne turned that way. Two guns were still roaring from somewhere behind the door. He glanced toward the entrance to the hall. Only darkness showed there.

He crossed the room and lifted the door latch. He pulled suddenly, stepping aside for an instant and then plunging into the room. He nearly stumbled over a man's body. As he caught himself, he saw Carnap. He had been taking aim at a curtained entryway at the far side of the room. He turned, bringing his gun around for a snap shot.

Marne's bullet caught him full in the face. His body slammed backwards, striking the curtain and ripping it down. Marne stared into a closet, at five tight faces. Squeezed against the wall behind Tonio were his relatives. He held a smoking gun, and his features were twisted with pain and anger.

"It is empty," he said, "or I would kill you." He stepped forward. "Do not kill them," he pleaded. "They have nothing to do with this."

"Stop being a jackass and let's get out of here," Marne snapped. "Your grandfather is guarding the back door, and Tim Killian has horses waiting." He glanced back at the dead man by the door. He was the one who had been standing guard in the kitchen.

"Where's the cook?"

"He ran away," Tonio said. He was staring at Marne.

"Load your gun and come on!" Marne ordered. "Only Doncaster and Rutter are here now, but the crews will ride in any minute."

Tonio's grandmother stepped briskly forward. "Why do you stand there, *nieto?*" Her tone was the same she would have used toward a small child, and Marne saw Tonio flush.

Tonio stepped forward and stumbled over Carnap. The sight of the body seemed to bring him back to complete awareness. "*Vámonos!*" he said sharply.

Marne turned. "I'll go out first. You bring up the rear."

The boys darted forward suddenly. One of them caught

up Carnap's gun. The other took the .44 from the other dead man. "Between us," one of them ordered the women.

Tonio's grandmother demanded one of the guns. All four of them began arguing in voluble Spanish. Marne swallowed a desire to swear and started out of the room. Glancing back, he saw that they were coming after him. The boys still held on to the guns.

Death lay all around them; yet, somehow they never quite seemed to believe it would touch them personally, Marne thought. In a whisper, he told them to stop for a moment. He stepped into the kitchen, his eyes probing at the hall door. There was no one. He frowned, wondering where Rutter and Doncaster were. One of them had followed him outside, but where was the other?

His answer came in a burst of gunfire. His ear caught the heavy boom of two .44's and the sharper crack of a rifle. He raced for the doorway. Darkness engulfed him and then cleared as he reached the moonlight. Gunfire was blossoming from the bunkhouse to his left. At first he couldn't locate the target. Then he saw the sheriff crouched behind the watering trough a dozen feet beyond the veranda steps.

"Stay back!" Marne whispered to those inside. He broke into a diving run that carried him alongside Potrero.

"They're all safe," he whispered in Spanish. "Give Killian the signal."

"There are two by the bunkhouse," the sheriff answered. "They will see the horses and kill them, and perhaps Lieutenant Killian as well."

"We have to get your people away before the crews start coming in," Marne said. "And Tonio has a new wound. He needs doctoring." He stared at the bunkhouse. "Give your signal and start shooting again. I'll try and get on Doncaster's flank and keep him and Rutter off balance."

Keeping to shadow, Marne worked back to the house and ran alongside it. When he heard the sheriff start shooting again, he broke into the moonlight-splashed open yard and sprinted for the rear of the bunkhouse. If either Doncaster or Rutter chose to glance his way, they couldn't miss seeing him—or miss the target he made. He ran faster, straining for the safety of deep shadow.

He was almost there when he caught the jangle of harness, the beat of hoofs. He turned and saw riders outlined in the moonlight. Some of the hands were back! At least a dozen, Marne guessed. And they were no more than five minutes away. If they heard the gunfire, they would run their horses and be here well before that time.

There was no time now to slip up on Doncaster and Rutter. He had to make some kind of a move that would distract the crew as well as them.

He studied the landscape. Moonlight fell harshly everywhere now. Only the buildings—the house, the bunkhouse, the barns—threw strong shadows.

The barns! A grim chuckle surged up into Marne's throat. That was the answer. The nearest barn was a hundred feet away, and to reach it he would have to run through the moonlight. It was possible one of the riders would see him and wonder, perhaps even sound an alarm. He took a deep breath and raced away from the protection of the bunkhouse wall.

The sheriff had stopped shooting. But now he started again, telling Marne that Killian was drawing close. Two guns answered from the front of the bunkhouse. Now Marne could see the riders lift the pace of their horses. Even so, they seemed to be moving slowly, as if the animals were too tired to find any speed in themselves.

But they were closing in quickly now. Someone shouted and Marne knew he had been seen. The same voice rose again, demanding to know who he was. Marne plunged for shadow lying ahead. A rifle cracked, sending lead scouring the ground near him. He felt the blackness wrap itself around him. Another rifle sent a bullet into the barn wall. A third cracked angrily. Marne found the barn door, lifted the heavy bar holding the door leaves together, and threw himself inside.

Two more minutes, he thought. That was all he needed.

And even that might be too much time for Tim Killian and the horses.

Marne found a lantern and lit it. He stared around at the piles of wooden cases. They were familiar sights—boxes of guns and ammunition, originally packed for the army, for a war that was still not quite ended.

He moved quickly around the great room. In a far corner, he found what he sought: cans of coal oil. Quickly, he opened one and splashed it on the wooden walls, on the sides of the boxes holding guns and ammunition for them. He retreated to the door, letting a trail of coal oil follow him. The stench began to fill the room. He could feel it working at his eyes, at his head. He struck a match and threw it at the damp trail he had made. It flickered, caught, and flame leaped up. Marne swung the lantern against the wall, shattering the glass. Flame from its wick caught eagerly at the coal oil soaked wood.

Marne flung the barn doors wide to let air flood in. He sprinted out, turning for the corner to his right. The riders were almost to the yard now. Two rifles searched for him as he flung himself around the corner.

A voice cried, "Fire! The barn's on fire!"

Marne ran upslope for the trees. Behind him he heard the cessation of firing from the front of the bunkhouse. Doncaster's voice raised in questioning and then broke as flames leaped out of the barn door.

Men began shouting incoherent orders. The barn was burning fiercely now, sending flames shooting high, lighting the yard as clearly as if day had come. Marne reached a point even with the rear of the bunkhouse. He stopped and looked down.

Doncaster was in the middle of the yard. He was pointing toward six fleeing riders and one horse with an empty saddle. "The devil with the barn. It's too late to stop it now. Get fresh horses and go after them! Burn the town if you have to, but get them all."

He turned, running for the corral. Rutter came after him, more slowly, moving like a man hurt. Doncaster stopped.

"I'll pay five hundred dollars to the man who brings me Marne's carcass!

"Now move!"

XVIII

MARNE WATCHED the group led by Killian disappear into the darkness under the trees. A few riders sent futile shots after them, but most of the CR men were running for the corral.

"Hurry up before that powder starts to go off!" someone shouted. The riflemen turned and ran, leaving Doncaster and Rutter to follow them more slowly.

Flames leaped high now, throwing brightness over the yard and the slope beyond it. The roar of the fire grew until all other sounds were drowned by it. Marne began to run, hoping to reach the Arroyo Verde people before they left with his horse. He slowed as a rider came toward him, moving just beyond the edge of the firelight. It was Tim Killian, and he was leading the dun.

"I thought we'd never find you after that barn started to burn," he said. "I saw you go in there but I was too busy to see you come out."

Marne climbed gratefully into the saddle. "Doncaster has a dozen men getting ready to ride," he said. "One of us had better get the people back to town. The other one should go to Marita before she stumbles onto the CR crew."

Flames leaping high threw light on Killian's face. Marne saw how drawn, how drained of blood and strength he was. "Get back to Marita," he ordered. "And make it fast." He paused and added, "And have her dress that wound again. From the looks of you, it's opened up."

"You'll need all the help you can get making an army out of the townspeople," Killian said.

"Having you to nurse won't make the job any easier," Marne snapped. "Now ride. And that's an order, Lieutenant."

If Killian remembered his earlier remark that Marne had no jurisdiction since he was on leave, he didn't bother to repeat it now. With a tight salute, he reined his horse and spurred it into the darkness and out of sight, taking a different route to his camp.

Marne looked down at the yard. Mounted men were coming from the corral now. Fresh horses and angry gunmen, Marne thought. And led by a madman. For he knew that even though Doncaster had kept himself rigidly under control these last moments, inside he must be torn by violent hatred. His demand for Marne's body had shown that.

His pride had been mocked, the main reason for his life threatened. And by an army man—a Captain of a Yankee army!

Marne saw him appear. He rode his pale golden horse, a cavalry officer ready to call the charge. With a sweep of his hand, he brought Rutter on his black alongside. Together, they led the men around the house and out of sight. They were taking the main trail to Arroyo Verde, Marne guessed. It was no longer, but with its fewer turns and hills, it would be faster for fresh horses. With two women and Tonio wounded, the sheriff's little group would make poor time.

Marne put his heels to the dun as he realized that Doncaster would reach town first, that he would most likely have control of it before the sheriff and his people arrived.

Suddenly the earth seemed to split apart. The sky shattered as if the moon had exploded. Marne was well into the trees but even so he could see the great gouts of flame and smoke leaping up, and metal from bursting shells and bullets whined over his head. The ammunition had finally gone up.

A great chunk of brass struck a tree to Marne's left. The dun panicked, leaping forward and crashing through a stand of scrub piñon. Marne hung on grimly until they were in the open again. He managed to calm the horse and set it to wearing out its fear on the trail.

The sheriff's group was well ahead. Marne did not catch a glimpse of them until he was at the junction of the two small gullies. He was about to call out when he saw that everyone had stopped. A shout arose, and as he drew near, he heard Marita cry out her grandmother's name in pleasure and relief.

"Then the Señor Marne succeeded," Marita said. "But—where is he?"

The sheriff said heavily, "We saw him set fire to one of the barns—so that we might escape. Killian went to find him but they have not come back."

"Tim! He is back there?"

Marne hurried the dun up to the small group. "Hold it," he told her. "Killian's gone back to his camp."

A babble of sound rose as they realized who he was. Marne stilled it quickly. "There is no time now," he said. "Marita, take the women and Tonio and get back to the camp. Tonio and Killian both need help."

He swung on the sheriff. "Doncaster and his crew took the main road. They'll have control of the town before we get within rifle distance."

The meaning of Marne's words struck the old man. His shoulders sagged. "We ride too slowly," he said. "Now Doncaster will take our people again—the *padre*, our friends, perhaps even the children. We cannot fight him."

"There's a chance," Marne said. He didn't tell them how slender a chance it was. "But we can't do anything staying here and talking." He looked pointedly at Tonio. "Nor can we do anything if we have to worry about wounded men."

"I will go with Marita," Tonio said in a low voice.

Marne didn't believe him. But there was no time for argument now. Leaving Marita with the women and Tonio, he led the sheriff and the two boys up the trail. The sheriff came alongside him at a wide stretch.

"Your words are brave," he said in Spanish, "but how much truth is in them?"

Marne said, "I wasn't lying. We do have a chance. Doncaster wants me more than he wants anything right now. I'll give him the chance to catch me. If I can pull him and enough of his men after me, you might be able to get to some of your people."

116

THE HOLDOUT IN THE DIABLOS

"We cannot let you sacrifice yourself, Señor Marne."

"I don't intend to," Marne said dryly. "Here's my plan."
He spoke quickly. The sheriff listened in silence.

When Marne finished, he said softly, "Sí, it is a chance.
But if we are late . . . if something should go wrong . . ."

"Let's figure it won't," Marne said. He put his heels to the
dun, sending the compact little animal hurtling up the moon-
lit trail.

When he neared Arroyo Verde, he slowed the horse. Finding a vantage spot, he looked down on the scatter of lights.
But there was no noise, no sound of Doncaster's conquering
army rising from the little village. Puzzled, Marne was about
to start away when he saw them coming.

He wondered why they had taken so long, and then he
realized that instead of a dozen men, Doncaster now had
over twenty. He had taken the time to round up more of his
remaining crews. That could only mean he was planning an
all-out war—on Marne, on Killian, on the people of Arroyo
Verde.

Shadow swallowed the steadily moving men. Then they
rode again into bright moonlight. Doncaster led, with Rutter
close behind him. Marne watched only long enough to see
that they intended riding straight into the town. Doncaster
would not bother to deploy his forces. In his arrogance, he
would presume that he could simply go in and take over.

Marne sent the dun back to the trail he had been riding.
He came to the rear of the posada, hunted the area until he
found the end of the tunnel he had ridden through earlier,
and then turned to meet Doncaster and his men.

He saw them moving through the plaza. His eyes glinted
and his mouth tipped up in a grin as he leaned forward and
sent the dun hurtling into the open. He drew his gun and
shouted, "Hold it right there, Doncaster!"

Doncaster reined up, staring in surprise. Behind him Tink's
familiar voice crowed, "It's that army man!"

His gun went off, sending lead whining close to Marne.
Twisting only slightly in the saddle, Marne answered the

117

shot, driving his bullet close to Rutter. Tink cried out in wonderment and seemed to fling himself out of the saddle.

Marne turned back. "The next one's for you, Doncaster." As he talked, he sidled the dun, moving it into the edge of shadow, near the alley mouth he wanted.

Behind Doncaster a gun hammer snicked as it was drawn back. "Hold your fire, you fools!" he commanded. He leaned forward. "What can you gain by this, Marne? Kill me and twenty guns will cut you to nothing."

Marne and the dun were blending deeper and deeper into the darkness. "A smart man would surrender," he answered. "I don't want your twenty men; I only want you. But if I have to, I'll get rid of every one that has the courage to stand between us."

It was a windy speech, he knew, and he had trouble controlling his laughter as he spoke it. Then the desire to laugh died as Doncaster flattened himself over his horse's neck and sent the animal leaping wildly to one side.

"Get him!" he cried. "Five hundred dollars to the man that brings me his hide! Remember that!"

Marne held his fire. He would have shot at Doncaster if he could have been sure of not hitting him. But he wanted Doncaster alive, and trying to miss a moving man was too great a risk. He turned the dun and sent it flying into the alley. Guns opened up behind him, sending lead smashing into the adobe walls near by, sending it whispering over Marne's head, sending it searching for him through the darkness.

He tried to force the dun to a faster pace. He could feel the small horse tremble and he realized how far he had ridden it this day. "Not far now, fellow," he said softly. "Just a little way past the posada here."

He turned and looked back. Doncaster's men were streaming after him, fanning out in a wide arc. They were trying to make a circle with Marne as the centerpoint.

With their still relatively fresh horses, the CR crew moved faster than the dun could manage. Marne judged the distance he had yet to go. Before, he had figured his chances of reaching safety at better than even. Now he wasn't so sure.

The dun stumbled, caught itself, and slowed to a jog. A few more feet and it stopped, head hanging, legs spraddled wih weariness.

Marne had no choice. Pulling his carbine from the boot, he dropped to the ground and began to run. Behind him someone shouted and he knew he had been seen.

He ran on.

XIX

BUSHES AND SMALL trees threw shadows close to the side of the posada. Marne burrowed his way into the darkness and dropped to his knees. In this position, he was able to crawl under the tree limbs that brushed the rough adobe wall of the building. Slowly, with agonizing pauses to listen for the sounds of pursuit, Marne made his way toward the rear yard and possible safety.

Whichever CR man had spotted him before, he had lost Marne now. The same voice was shouting angrily, insisting he had seen their quarry. Marne chuckled as he listened to the disagreement. A few wanted to believe he had been seen. Others wanted to spread out and search this entire section of town rather than just the posada yard.

"He's probably being hid inside," one man shouted. "I say break down the door and have us a look!"

Marne swore as others took up the cry. He could imagine what would happen to Pablo and Elena, to the servants, if these angry, excited gunmen invaded their refuge.

Marne rose and peered out through the bushes. The CR crew was knotted into what appeared a shapeless mass of horses and men. All of them seemed more interested in the argument as to their next move than in looking about for Marne. He stepped into the open and began to move slowly

119

parallel to the posada wall. He was still in shadow and he was almost to the far corner of the building before he heard the shout that told he had been seen again.

In another moment he would have shouted to draw their attention, to bring them after him instead of going into the posada. But now there was no need. Men were reining their horses about. Others were cursing because in the tight knot there was no room to maneuver. Marne paused, turned and sent two shots from his carbine screaming at the CR crew. The first he sent into the ground nearest the hoofs of the horse closest to him; the second he put over the tallest rider's head.

A horse reared as the bullet ricocheted near it. Marne fired a third time, sending dirt and rock spinning upward. A second horse pawed at the sky. Its rider grabbed leather, swearing wildly. Panic runs through horses as swiftly as through humans, Marne knew. He sprinted across the yard and plunged into shadow near a spreading juniper. As he had hoped, the excitement the two frightened horses were generating was spreading to the others.

Someone went down. A second rider broke free of the knot of men and milling horses and charged toward the rear yard, at the point where Marne had last been seen.

This was what he had been waiting for. He tensed himself and took a step into the open. "Looking for me?" he called softly.

The rider was close enough to hear him. He swung his horse about. Marne laughed with pleasure. The rider was Tink. He held the reins in his left hand, awkwardly because his arm was in a crude sling. His .44 was in his right fist. He lifted it, skinning back his teeth in pure hatred.

Marne shot him out of the saddle, lifting the carbine barrel and firing from the hip. Two strides carried him to the horse, poised as if it would bolt at any further violence. Marne hauled himself into the saddle. The shot had brought other men swirling out of the knot. A man shouted, "There he goes!"

Lead searched the darkness. Marne heard it whisper past

his head, felt the tick of it against his bootheel, caught its deadly breath blowing at the brim of his hat. He flattened himself in the saddle and put his heels to Tink's horse.

Marne's urging, and a bullet that scoured its rump, sent the animal surging toward the rough ground at the rear of the well kept yard. Marne turned and looked back. The knot had come completely untied now and close to twenty men were streaming after him. He weaved the horse as gunfire began to come closer to its target. Then the yard ended and the rough canyon country began. Marne made a sharp right swing and reined in the horse. The first pursuers went by the mouth of the small canyon he had entered.

Marne lifted his rifle and sent a shot howling over the head of the third man to ride past. The man turned. He shouted, "This way!" and answered Marne's shot with one that went hopelessly wide.

Marne reined the horse around and raced it up the canyon. But as he neared the entrance to the tunnel, he slowed. A glance behind showed him that the CR crew was well back, and he kept his pace down until they began to catch up. Then, as he turned the horse into the tunnel, he fired one last shot to make sure that he was seen.

He pushed the horse forward a short distance and then reached out cautiously. His hand hit the cold, rough wall, fumbled, and found the rope that had guided Marita through earlier. He stopped the horse and listened.

He laughed softly. "Horse, your friends back there aren't very much on brains," he murmured. The CR riders were doing as he had hoped—and expected. Wild with anger because of the chase he had led them, because of the almost mocking way he had eluded them, they had streamed into the tunnel behind him. Now he could hear some of them cursing as they realized the depths of the darkness that enfolded them.

"Get back! It's a trap."

"Watch out, you fool. Do you want to trample me to death?"

"By God, let me out of here!"

Marne listened to the sound of horses being turned, being ridden too fast for safety toward the open air. He held himself rigidly, praying that the sheriff had managed his end of the job. Then he heard a familiar voice:

"That's far enough, hombres! Any man that comes out here comes with his gunbelt missing, his hands in the air, and leading his horse."

A gun cracked, punctuating the command. Marne shook his head. That was Tim Killian out there. But he should have known that the Lieutenant wouldn't stay out of the fight, not as long as he was able to cling to his saddle.

Men began to curse. Marne called, "Ride this way, boys. Just keep going and you'll get out—if you don't get lost first."

He started up the horse, moving slowly enough to keep his hand on the guide rope. The sounds behind him began to fade. But he heard more than one voice cry, "I'm coming out. Hold your fire!" and he knew that before long Killian and whoever was with him would have a corral full of prisoners.

So far so good, Marne thought. What had seemed disaster when the dun quit on him had turned to possible success—if things went as well at the other end of the tunnel as they had at this end.

He would know soon. He felt rough rock as the rope bent around a sharp angle. Then a lighter patch showed ahead, and before long he could see moonlight.

"Just be there, sheriff," Marne murmured. He reached the tunnel's end and sent the horse stepping briskly into the cool, fresh air.

A voice said, "Hold your fire! That's Tink's horse."

"That ain't Tink on top of it, by God!"

Marne turned. Doncaster's big golden animal and Rutter's black stood by the corner of the church. Their riders had carbines aimed at the mouth of the tunnel. Behind them, hands held high, were Marita and Tonio. Smitty had his horse broadside to the pair so that he could hold his .44 easily on both of them.

"It's Marne!" Rutter said thickly.

"So I expected," Doncaster replied. He leaned forward

without taking his gun from its position. "We almost rode into your trap at the other end of the tunnel too, Marne, but we pulled back in time."

Marne said, "So you figured out what I was up to and came here as a welcoming committee."

"Let's say we're a delegation with a request." The pleasant, mocking tone Doncaster had been using fell away. His voice became cold. "We're going back to your friend. You're going to tell him to turn my men loose. Then both of you are coming with us—back to the CR."

Marne said, "And if I tell you to go to hell? What then? Why should I ride all the way back to the CR to let you shoot me? I'd rather you did it now."

"If I have to shoot you now, your two friends here will go along with you."

"In that case, I'll ride," Marne answered dryly. He reined the horse in a half turn to the right, as if he were going to carry out Doncaster's instructions. He had put his carbine back in the boot during his time in the tunnel, but his right hand lay on his leg close to his .44.

He seemed to explode. His hand whipped to the butt of his gun. He drew, twisted about, fired at Smitty, and flattened in the saddle in one fluid movement.

Smitty jerked up and back. Tonio whooped and started his horse forward. Marne cried, "Get Marita out of here!" in Spanish and then he was hurtling Tink's horse straight at Doncaster and Rutter, firing as he went.

Both men were trying to bring their horses around to get into position to answer the charge. Rutter never finished his turn. His first shot whipped close to Marne's head. His second screamed almost straight into the air as Marne's .44 bullet drove him out of the saddle. He struck the ground, rolled once, and lay still.

Doncaster's carbine found the range. Marne felt the sharp bite of a bullet crashing into his left shoulder. The force of the blow sent him half out of the saddle. He recovered and fired as he came upright in the saddle. Doncaster cursed as for the second time in a few short days Marne's aim was dead on target. The carbine was ripped from his hand and sent spinning out of reach.

Doncaster swung his magnificent horse and drove it straight at Marne. The distance between them was too short for Marne to risk shooting at Doncaster. At most, he wanted only to wound the man. But a slight move on Doncaster's part and the bullet meant to put him out of action could put him in the grave instead.

The big golden animal under Doncaster crashed into Tink's lighter horse. Marne felt the jolt tear at his throbbing shoulder. He made an effort to swing the horse away, to give himself room to maneuver. But Doncaster was driving his solid body forward, kicking himself free of the saddle and climbing onto the dun. His fingers caught Marne around the neck in a murderous grip.

Marne had a swift glimpse of Doncaster's face, of the wildness there, of the crazed anger that was driving him to this final effort. Then Doncaster's features blurred as the power of his grip choked off Marne's wind and sent the blood dancing behind his eyes.

He made an effort to shake Doncaster free, but he managed only to send pain cascading up through his bullet-torn shoulder. He lifted his right arm and slashed the barrel of his gun at Doncaster's head. Despite his agony he sought to control the blow, to keep from crushing in the man's skull—and the effort cost him the gun. Doncaster leaned away from it, lifted one hand long enough to jerk it from Marne's fingers, and then grunted as it slipped away to the ground.

Marne clawed at Doncaster's wrist. But Doncaster was the fresher, the stronger at this moment. And his madness seemed to give him a wild strength that nothing could stop. He brushed Marne's arm aside and closed both hands again around Marne's neck.

Once more his wind was cut off. Once more blood began to dance behind his eyes. He could feel consciousness slipping away, and the more he fought, the quicker the strength drained out of him.

With a final effort, Marne brought his right fist up and

smashed it against Doncaster's temple. The gripping fingers slipped slightly. Marne struck again. A third time.

And now he could breathe as Doncaster lost his grip and had to reach for it again.

Marne sucked deep draughts of chill air into his aching lungs. His head began to clear and he could feel strength flowing into his muscles. As Doncaster's fingertips brushed his throat, he sent his fist forward in a final, smashing blow full into Doncaster's face. He felt cartilage and bone give under the force of his fist. Doncaster's eyes widened with shock, and the madness began to drain out of them. He began to tip sideways, slowly at first, but then faster until his balance was gone. He crashed to the dirt and lay quietly in the cloud of thin dust puffing up around him.

Marne half stepped, half fell from the horse. He said wonderingly, disbelievingly, "Two damn years!" and then he stumbled and sprawled across the body.

He knew that he should move, that there were things yet to be done. But somehow they didn't seem to matter. Somehow he wanted only this soothing, enveloping darkness.

The smell of rich coffee and the soft liquid sounds of Spanish voices opened Marne's eyes. Sunlight streamed through a window, touching the bed where he lay. His shoulder was bulky with a thick bandage and his face felt damp, as if it had just been washed.

He glanced to his right and saw Tim Killian stretched on a bed only a few feet away. Near him Tonio was propped in a chair, his feet held high by a bench.

"Welcome to the base hospital, Captain," Killian said.

Marita moved into view, carrying a tray loaded with cups of steaming coffee. Marne said, "What happened? Where's Doncaster?"

"In the *calabozo*," Killian replied. "The sheriff put him there right after he picked you up."

Marita nodded and set a cup of coffee on a small table by Marne's right hand. He saw that his tobacco and pouch were already there. "The *abuelo* will be in soon to tell you everything, *capitán*. But everything is all right. The men were captured as you planned. All of them—even those who were still in the hills when the fighting took place. And our people are guarding the barns at the *rancho*." Her glance touched Killian softly. "Tim says that it is now the property of the government."

Killian coughed. "Ah, Captain, I understand that a few of the smaller items—ones that didn't get burned—have disappeared. We can't be sure, of course, since there was no inventory, but things like sidearms and carbines, ammunition, harness and other gear, food . . ."

Marne thought of the Arroyo Verde people, living out their lives on slender rations, on the edge of poverty, suddenly finding what must be a treasure to them.

He said, "As you said, Lieutenant, there was no inventory. Just make sure they leave the cannon and a few wagons—to make Washington happy."

His voice had taken on a formal, military tone. It grew even stiffer as he added, "I want Doncaster to be treated the way any officer who is a prisoner of war should be treated. I want no charges of irregularities laid against us at his trial."

"You saved him for that trial," Killian said. "May I ask why, sir?"

Marne said readily, "Doncaster represents a dream that men like him should have wakened from years ago. Such men are trying to bring back a past that died in April, eight years back. I want them to know what happened to Doncaster. Dead, he's nothing—a martyr for a short time, nothing more. But alive, tried and hanged—he's a sermon."

He reached for his coffee. "And, Lieutenant, you might be surprised to discover how many unbelievers hearing that sermon suddenly find themselves interested in salvation."

Setting down his cup, he picked up his pipe and pouch. Soon he was sending a cloud of strong smoke toward Killian. "When is the wedding, Lieutenant?"

Killian flushed. "Why, sir, we hadn't talked about it . . ."

In Spanish, Marne asked Marita the same question. She

came back quickly, smiling, with, *"Lo antes, lo mejor, capitán."*

Killian looked puzzled. "My Spanish isn't quite up to that, sir."

Marne said, "Then have the lady teach you. Meanwhile, you can regard her remark as an order."

Behind Killian, Tonio was grinning broadly. Marne answered with a grin of his own and then discreetly turned his face the other way as Marita bent toward Killian, whispering to him.

Killian said, "Yes, sir! That *is* an order. The sooner the better!"

Marne chuckled, rolled over, and reached for his coffee cup.

Louis Trimble was born in Seattle, Washington, and during most of his professional career taught in the University of Washington system of higher education. 'I began writing Western fiction,' he later observed, 'because of my interest in the history and physical character of the western United States and because the Western was (and is) a genre in which a writer could move with a great deal of freedom.' His first Western novel under the Louis Trimble byline was *Valley of Violence* (1948). In this and his subsequent Western novels he seems to have been most influenced by Ernest Haycox, another author who lived in the Pacific Northwest. He also used the *nom de plume* **Stuart Brock** under which he wrote five exceptional Westerns, all published by Avalon Books in the 1950s. The point of focus in his Western fiction, whether he is writing as Louis Trimble or Stuart Brock, constantly shifts among various viewpoints and women are often major characters. *Railtown Sheriff* (1949) was Trimble's first Western novel as Stuart Brock and it was under this byline that some of his most exceptional work appeared, most notably *Action at Boundary Peak* and *Whispering Canyon*, both in 1955, and *Forbidden Range* in 1956. These novels have strong characters, complex and realistic situations truly reflecting American life on the frontier, and often there is a mystery element that heightens a reader's interest. The terrain of the physical settings in these stories is vividly evoked and is an essential ingredient in the narrative. Following his retirement from academic work, Trimble made his retirement home in Devon, England.